Drifting and Other Stories

Drifting and Other Stories

Steven Faulkner

RESOURCE *Publications* • Eugene, Oregon

DRIFTING AND OTHER STORIES

Resource Publications
An Imprint of Wipf and Stock Publishers
199 W. 8th Ave., Suite 3
Eugene, OR 97401

www.wipfandstock.com

PAPERBACK ISBN: 979-8-3852-6907-5
HARDCOVER ISBN: 979-8-3852-6908-2
EBOOK ISBN: 979-8-3852-6909-9

VERSION NUMBER 02/09/26

Cover design by Seth Faulkner.

Illustrations by Steven Faulkner.

For Jasper Fox

Contents

Words with the Tomten

Alpha, the fifteen-year-old, climbed the ladder that led to the corridor above; his eight-year-old brother followed. As Alpha's head rose above the floorboards, he stopped to check the weather, peering out the transparent but faded plastique fiber of the corridor that connected the living area bubble on his right to the communications unit twenty feet to his left. The hardened plastique on the windward side was arched to lessen wind resistance, but twenty years of blowing grit and sand had frosted the surface, blurring his vision of the dry landscape, though he could still see the deep-red ridgeline of rock freshly illuminated by the sun rising behind him. It seemed to be a clear, quiet morning. No dust storms. No wind.

He climbed onto the floorboards and turned toward Communications, a carbon-fiber unit with a dome of tempered glass and a single round side window that looked out on what used to be a clear carbon-fiber-enclosed garden. Eight-year-old Beta followed his older brother up the ladder and turned in the opposite direction toward the living area.

They were the second generation to live on Mars, the first two born on the planet. The only two still alive.

Alpha, dark-haired, strong, genetically controlled to be a commander, walked to the Communications door, turned the handle, and pulled. The airtight door opened with a wheezing sound. He walked in, pulled the door shut behind him, and took his place in the worn chair before the large, blank screen.

His finger hit the Reporting Button. A tiny green light appeared on the console but the screen, as always, remained black. He got up and stepped to the round side window. Twenty feet beyond the window he could see, as always, half covered in sand and grit, the baked and torn space suits that still contained his parents' bones. On a day of ordinary winds, ragged shreds of their suits would be flapping, sometimes revealing a section of dry yellow bone, but today the dirt and fabric lay still.

He put out his thumb and traced the sign of a cross on the tempered glass, leaving on the glass a scratched cross years in the making. Alpha was no longer religious, but making the sign had always seemed the right symbol to honor his mother.

His parents' generation had built a construction unit nearby where they had made these glass windows and the observation dome. There was plenty of sand with which to make glass, but the carbon fiber panels that enclosed Communications and the transparent plastique surrounding the corridor, living areas, and garden had been lighter and more easily transported from Earth. The construction experts had left soon after building the place 20 years ago. The glass-making facility, a quarter of a mile away, had been shut down. Once the farming unit was self sufficient, the Space Agency had intended to use the factory as a base for mining operations: rare metals depleted on Earth had been discovered here in layers of rock.

Sometimes at night Alpha would waken from a dream of the thunderous explosion that had killed his parents, shattering the half-acre farming bubble, exposing their scorched, broken bodies to the unbreathable atmosphere of Mars. His father and mother had been wearing their space suits because they had been moving in and out of the double airlock bringing in buckets of reddish dirt and sand. They had been mixing Mars dirt with the Earth soil that covered the carbon-fiber flooring in the farming bubble. Within hours of the explosion, the genetically modified beans and corn and potatoes, and the new strawberries and broccoli and cabbage plants that had looked so promising had all been scorched, shriveled, and blown away. Not a leaf left.

Alpha's little brother Beta had been two years old at the time of the explosion, so Alpha, nine at the time, had that day become a single parent, learning quickly to microwave adult foods from the diminishing stacks of plastic-packaged dinners and to grind and boil Mars-grown corn and beans and potatoes, then spoon them into little Beta's mouth. He had mixed the powdered goat milk brought from Earth with water, added a little organic sweetener as his mother had taught him, and warmed the bottle in the microwave unit. Within three or four weeks, the little dark-eyed baby had finally stopped his incessant crying for Momma, but for days thereafter the two-year-old wouldn't let Alpha out of his sight, crawling rapidly after him and howling every time Alpha tried to leave the living area. Alpha would shout at the baby to stay, but this did no good. He had taken his mother's backsack and had begun carrying the boy around as he made the daily inspections of the living units.

Now Alpha turned the door handle, pushed open the wheezing door, stepped out of Communications, turned to push the door till it clicked shut, then made his way down the corridor toward the living area.

When he walked into the cooking unit, eight-year-old Beta was already boiling corn and beans that had been soaking all night in water taken from the WR, the water recycler. Beta, as always, sprinkled sweetener onto his cereal and added powdered goat milk. Alpha sprinkled the powdered milk on his bowl of cereal too, but mixed in a little salt instead of sugar.

They ate in silence.

They placed their two bowls and spoons, as well as the cooking pot in the cleaning unit and started their rounds: Maintenance Mornings.

Little Beta walked the perimeter looking for surface infractions, loose connections, any visible or audible trouble, while Alpha made his way to the underground engineering unit beneath the communications module and checked the gauges and listened to the machinery.

The communications system had blinked out just two months after the explosion. He had no idea why. The electronics seemed to be functional, and his nine-year-old fingers had tapped out the messages informing Earth that his parents had died and that he and his brother were still alive. Earth had promised quick relief, but after electronics had shut down, no message had arrived from Earth now for over six years. Maybe something had happened on Earth. A war. Some malfunction. A change in priorities. Who knew, but it seemed worth it to punch the Reporting Button on the off chance that someone out there was listening. No resupply ships had appeared since the year before their parents died, but he still hoped one night to be peering up through the clear dome of Communications into the starry sky and see an approaching flame. It was, after all, their only hope. In four or five years, their food supplies would be gone and they would starve. Or, more likely, the WR would break down and they would die of thirst. Or the electronics would blink out and the oxygenator, the lights, the heating and cooling units, everything would halt, making for rapid death, or

. . . there was an almost endless list of possible disasters. His hopes having eroded, Alpha tried to focus on daily tasks.

After lunch they would move to the exercise machines and work out for an hour. Alpha used to create competitive games on the exercise machines to get Beta to work hard, but in time Beta figured out that Alpha was only pretending to lose those games once in a while, and Beta lost interest. After that came Afternoon Activities, a time for pursuing one's own interests, but this was a problem. The computerized library had died the day of the explosion, so there was little entertainment for a couple of boys. His mother had brought one thin children's book from Earth when they immigrated: a picture book she had never read to Alpha since the computerized library had been vast and they would watch stories play out on the big screen as his mother read to them; the stories were timed to her speech and would stop when she stopped reading to pick up Beta or give him his bottle. But now the stories were long gone, and they were both left with nothing but water, food, shelter.

Most afternoons Beta would draw pictures on the erasable drawing pads; he was getting good at line drawings and coloring while Alpha would work out new melodies and chords on his mother's old guitar.

The shelter was a series of connected units housing the necessities: electronics, communications, protected solar panels, an underground storage unit, the engineering unit that held the vital machinery beneath Communications, and two underground, connected bedrooms. Beyond their shelter, toward sundown, was a ridge of stone that was meant to be something of a wind break. In every other direction they looked out on a vast, blank desert that ran away for 50 miles to an indistinct horizon. On a clear day they could sometimes make out a thin line of pale blue hills to the east fading and appearing and disappearing, depending on atmospheric conditions and wind. Often dust and sandstorms would blast over the western ridgeline and they could barely see the solar panels unit fifty feet away.

Beta, being two when the video library disappeared, remembered nothing of those fantastic views of Earth's mountains with their green forests, leaping mountain goats, bugling elk, swimming moose, and wandering cougars, dense jungles with monkeys swinging hand over hand and brilliantly feathered birds, deserts choked with thorny plants and deadly snakes and other strange crawling creatures. His parents had come from a place they called Two-Son where, due to terrific thunderstorms, grey sheets of water literally fell from the skies in a myriad of tiny drops, a sight that had fascinated Alpha and left him yearning to feel the rain on his face, to smell it. In those movies, young Alpha had stared at massive white clouds rising thousands of feet into the air, and gazed as grey sheets of rain swerved down from the dark underbellies of the storm. Between the observer and the distant mountains was a rocky wasteland, but it, too, was filled with life. Tall saguaro cacti stood here and there across the rocky terrain: stiff, stoic beings that lifted arms to the skies, patiently asking for rain. Sometimes the movies showed huge carpets of wildflowers that had magically appeared out of desert soil as feathered flying creatures floated the air currents or hopped among the rocks. Two-Son deserts were nothing like the deserts of Mars. Nothing at all like Mars. The only clouds here were massive reddish dust storms that roared over the desert, obscuring the pale, pinkish skies. They could see the raging clouds rise above the ridgeline, building high into the sky, approaching like great monsters intent on tearing apart and trampling their tiny encampment.

Alpha often tried to remember the stories his mother had read. They were all Earth stories with their incredibly complicated settings which were almost impossible to relate to Beta who couldn't remember seeing the videos. Alpha had a hard time describing forests and oceans and snow-covered mountains to a boy who had only and always seen shades of red dirt, sand, and flat, wind-scoured rocks. Alpha's only visual aid was the thin kid's book called *The Tomten and the Fox.* Twenty nine pages of painted pictures, sprinkled with a few words that told a tale about a fox slipping into a Swedish farm on a cold, snowy night to kill hens, but the fox is stopped by the tomten, a short, skinny old dwarf no taller than the fox. The tomten's white beard hangs to his feet, his red stocking hat droops down his back. Apparently both the tomten and the fox know humanspeak, because the tomten talks to the fox, warning him away from the hens. Alpha assumed that foxes understood and spoke the English variety of humanspeak, though the only animal he remembered speaking in the stories his mother had read him was a colorful parrot who traveled around on the shoulder of a one-legged pirate. Of course there had been the many cartoon characters who could speak and sing and do crazy things, but he knew they weren't real.

The tomten warns the fox not to bother the hens. He takes a bowl of porridge the farm children leave outside every night for the tomten, and feeds the fox.

Beta, of course, had been fascinated by *Tomten and the Fox*. "What is snow?" he had asked.

"It's frozen water that turns to little white flakes and falls from the sky and then covers the trees and ground."

"Why?"

"Because it does."

"Does it taste sweet like our white sweetener?"

"It's chemically just water, but it's really cold."

"Why?"

"Once the temperatures drop below 0 degrees Celsius, liquid water magically turns to ice or snow."

"Like the ice in the refridge box?"

"Something like that."

"That's a lot cold. Why does the fox want to kill the hens?"

"It wants to eat them."

Beta was afraid of the two cows pictured sleeping in the barn, big animals with horns. He had never seen anything like them, but he loved the fox and thought it would be a very good idea if the fox were allowed to eat the chickens which looked strange with their long necks and bug eyes. Beta himself was really, really tired of boiled porridge, so he could understand the fox's appetite for chickens. Once or twice a week they opened one of the plastic-covered meals of chicken and rice, or lasagna, or beef stew, so Beta knew what chicken could taste like.

The little book was falling apart. By the time Beta was seven, he had the whole story memorized, all 484 words—if you counted the artist's signature on the last page and read the title page. Beta had even memorized the additional 105 words on the copyright page because Alpha had read every word of it every time just to make the story last longer. But now, since Beta had memorized the whole book, there was no point reading it to him anymore, though sometimes Beta still asked him to. It was, of course, about their only visual connection to Earth. When Alpha tried to describe different kinds of forests, he knew Beta visualized the sketchy depictions in the little book: impressionistic blobs and dots of color. Beta was fascinated by one picture of a great, leafless tree standing next to the grey wood of the farmhouse. Snow lay along its many grey, gaunt arms; it stood like a different version of the tall cacti Alpha had tried to describe.

The only plant that had survived the blast that killed their parents was their mom's foot-high orchid sitting on the kitchen table. Beta had taken over the careful watering of the plant once a week. Alpha had told him trees were like that but grew to be a hundred feet high. He had seen

Beta turn his eyes and stare at the pale red desert beyond their living area. Beta always turned to look out the sunrise side of the bubble because the prevailing winds had not frosted that side and they got a pretty clear view of the scattered flat rocks and red dirt that ran away for fifty miles to the hazy horizon. He thought his brother was trying in his mind to populate the whole plain with hundred-foot orchids.

One day Beta looked up from his orchid and said, "Which engineer invented the orchid?"

"What?"

"Who invented the orchid?"

"Nobody."

"What do you mean?" Beta looked at him.

"It just grew. Out of the ground, or I think Mom said they grow on trees down somewhere in the jungles."

"Jungles are a whole lot of really big trees covered with paper-like green plates of different sizes and shapes, right?"

"Right. They live where there's lots of rain and rivers." The only water Beta had ever seen was the stream that ran from the WR faucet and the water in the toilets. Alpha had drawn him crude pictures of rivers surrounded by penciled trees, but that wasn't much help. Beta loved the thought of running water and drew countless rivers, sometimes blue, sometimes pink, sometimes green.

"So nobody made this orchid?"

"Nobody made the corn and beans either. They just grew right out of the dirt, though Mom was really smart about making them grow better."

"Mom's orchid is alive, though, like us?"

"Yes."

"Why doesn't it breathe like us?"

"I don't know."

Beta reached out and touched one of the three flat, white flowers that had blossomed from the plant.

"I told you not to do that."

"They're soft."

"You know if you keep doing that it will fall apart like the tomten book."

"But it's alive. Won't it heal like we do when we scrape a knee?"

"It's a different life form. I don't know if it can heal."

"What is life?"

Alpha stood up to go. "I don't know, but it doesn't last long."

"But you said Earth is full of life. And it's lasted a long, long time."

Alpha stood there a moment. "It dies and wakes up, dies and wakes up."

"Will Mom and Dad wake up?"

"No."

"Why not?"

"Once the orchid dies, and it will soon if you keep messing with it, it's dead. Life wakes up from seeds, like corn and beans."

"Why?"

"Shut up, Beta. How am I supposed to know." He turned and walked away.

\+ + +

Every night Alpha would stop in Communications and punch the Reporting Button in case communication with Earth depended somehow on the angle of reception or the relative positions of Earth and Mars. Their electricity depended on the hundreds of hexagonal solar panels enclosed in a transparent tent-shaped structure made of hard plastique near their living quarters. The steep roof kept the sand and dirt from collecting and so far the electricity had been dependable. After punching the button, he would walk over to the window and perfunctorily thumb the cross. Mom had done that every morning after she and Dad had sent their daily report to Earth.

Alpha would then click off the lights in Communications, shut the door, walk eight steps to the ladder, climb down to their bedroom, and climb into the top bunk. Beta in the bottom bunk used to always ask for a bedtime story, but Alpha had run out of stories.

Their parents' bedroom was connected to theirs by a door, but he never went in there anymore.

He would try to sleep, but as a commander he was prone to worry. He had mathematically determined their likely life spans based on food depletion and probable mechanical breakdowns. He didn't expect they'd live more than three years. Probably a lot less.

Over the last week, his little brother had begun getting up in the night, climbing the ladder, and staying awake for hours. Alpha thought Beta would soon tire of this schedule because Alpha never let him sleep late in the mornings. But Beta didn't tire. So, one night Alpha climbed the ladder and found Beta sitting next to the clear eastern side of the bubble staring into darkness. The winds were blowing from behind them, occasionally kicking up a little sand, but they could still see the vast panorama of stars on the black sky.

"What are you doing?"

Beta had heard him coming, so he wasn't startled. "I'm watching for the tomten."

"There's no tomten here. That was just an Earth story."

"I saw something out there moving and I think it might be a real tomten."

"Beta, that's a story some guy made up."

"How about angels?

Alpha stopped to consider. Their mother had in fact believed in angels. The one artifact she had brought from earth besides her wooden guitar was a small, wooden Nativity set that she had carefully explained to Alpha: Mary and Joseph in carved robes, two sheep, an adult shepherd holding a long, hooked stick, a boy shepherd about the age of Alpha now, three kneeling "wise men" offering boxes to the lady, a camel with an elaborate saddle and reins, a donkey, and the baby holding up its little arms while lying in a rectangular wooden box stuffed with grass that their mom would replace every Christmas. Above the five-inch figures, attached to the peaked roof of the wooden stable, were two winged angels robed in white.

"Dad," said Alpha, "didn't believe angels exist, but you're right, Mom did." Alpha tended to agree with his father, but he didn't want to break this connection between his brother and their mother. Besides, their dad could have been wrong. He had been wrong about a hell of a lot of things: that Mars was a marvelous place where you could dependably grow your own food, that the dangers of living here were manageable, that he had the manuals (electronic and paper) for all the machinery and could fix anything, that the resupply ships would "most certainly return." After watching the story videos of Earth with his mother, this attitude had made Alpha angry, very angry—that anyone, for any reason whatsoever—would leave such a spectacular and beautiful planet to try to survive on this vast ball of dried dirt, baking rocks, blowing sand, and poisonous air.

Beta rubbed his skinny arms and said, "It's cold."

"I told you," said Alpha, "that we save energy by dropping the temperature at night in the living unit." He stood there and looked at Beta. "Why don't you come to bed?"

"I want to see the tomten. It was supposed to protect the little farm, wasn't it?"

"It protected the hens. We don't have hens."

"Aren't we worth more than hens?"

"Maybe."

"Then maybe there's an angel or something out there protecting us, maybe flying around. I saw some kind of shadow fly by tonight."

"It was just a dust cloud, Beta. You know that."

Alpha returned to the ladder and went to bed. He had told the Nativity story to Beta many times. It was the one story he could remember in detail, probably because he had visual aids. He had not told Beta the rest of that strange story. He couldn't figure out why a god would bother to come to Earth just to get himself murdered by his enemies, even if he did come back to life, and his mom had not really explained that part of the story because their dad didn't want her "filling their little heads with inventions," though she had told him that there were mysteries out there that we would never understand, and even Dad believed that. Speaking of mysteries, his first son thought that any race of beings who chose to leave a beautiful, habitable planet like Earth for a ridiculous place like Mars didn't understand even the basics of reality.

Their mother was an expert agronomist who had what she called a double P H D from a place called Kanzus State. His dad had told him she was a world-class, which meant Earth-class, genius when it came to plant growth and genetic modifications. She had been responsible for the success of the farm and Dad had been in charge of the machinery and living unit that supported the farming operation. Once the farming proved reliable, Earth was supposed to send engineers and miners to start extracting the rare earth minerals.

\+ \+ \+

Three or four nights later, Alpha climbed the ladder again and found Beta with a blanket wrapped around his skinny shoulders. He was talking to the darkness. He stopped talking when Alpha approached.

"What the hell are you doing?"

Beta sat still and stared into the darkness.

Alpha watched his brother for a minute or two, then walked back to Communications. He opened the wheezing door, took his seat on the worn-out plastic chair and pushed the button. The green light came on. The dark screen stared blindly into the darkness. Not even a flicker of light had ever appeared since the system crashed.

He peered up through the clear dome into the midnight sky. He picked up his binoculars, rested his elbows on the console, and found Earth. One light among countless lights. He raked the skies for any approaching flames.

In time, he returned to his bunk and fell asleep.

Beta didn't want to get up the next morning.

"Come on, kid! We've got work to do." He grabbed Beta's arm and pulled him to the floor.

Beta sighed, dressed, and followed Alpha up the ladder.

+ + +

Every night now, Alpha watched the skies from Communications. Every night Beta talked to the darkness. They began sleeping later and later, and spending more time watching the darkness. Often, one of the two moons of Mars would be up there reflecting a bit of sunlight. Sometimes a shooting star would leave a long yellow-red trail in its quick journey through the carbon dioxide atmosphere of Mars. Too often a sandstorm would rush over their living unit shaking the panels. Alpha, of course, worried about that. How long would it all hold together? On stormy nights when the star-heavy skies were shut away by blowing dust, Alpha would go back to bed, but Beta would stay in his chair and talk to the darkness. Once Alpha, returning to the ladder, heard him crying.

"Shut up, Beta!" he shouted down the corridor. "I miss them more than you do. You don't even remember them!" He climbed down the ladder and slid into bed.

+ + +

One night, with the wind sending a series of rasping gusts of sand and dirt against the hard plastique, he walked over to Beta, who was sitting at the kitchen table, and said, "Give it up, Beta! Nobody's going to answer you!"

"Then why don't you stop calling Earth?"

"Because it's our only possible hope! When I was your age, I saw a ship land, full of people and all kinds of supplies. We ate pears and apples for two months. They haven't forgotten us."

"The Reporting Button doesn't work," said Beta.

A strong gust of sand swept over the living bubble. He waited for the raspy, whispering, rattling sounds to subside.

"We don't know it doesn't work. They might be getting the messages but not be responding for some reason."

Alpha stared at his little brother. The wind blew, and the sand hissed over the living unit, and the panels squeaked and shook as the winds hurried eastward over that vast dark plain.

Beta looked up at his brother. "I think it's very strange that the orchid can just come to life like that."

"You are just as strange."

"Well, did we just pop out of seeds?"

"We popped out of Mom. That's what Dad said."

"That's crazy," Beta said. "He must have been joking."

"I don't think so. He was embarrassed and wouldn't explain it to me."

Beta stared at the orchid. "You said orchids and other life stuff grow out of dead seeds, so maybe growing out of Mom might not be crazy? Maybe she had a seed inside her?"

"Maybe."

"So how did the first seeds get started?"

"Dad told me it took millions of years for life to get rolling, as he put it."

"So time created the first seeds?"

"Time is not an active agent, it's a passive environment."

"What's an active agent?"

"Give it up, Beta. I suppose you think your tomten created the first seeds."

"How would I know?"

""If there is a tomten, he should be mad as hell that Mom and Dad left us here, living in a place like this. We can't even breathe the air out there. There's no water. No magnetic field, so the sun would fry us and give us all kinds of cancers. I'd be mad as hell if I"d given a single stream of water and a small group of trees and a little scrap of earth to Mom and Dad, and air to breathe and crops to harvest, and they left it to come here. Mom used to sing that song about a place like that, remember?"

"I don't remember Mom."

"I know! I know! But you've heard me sing it. He started reciting the song: 'Now as I was young and easy/ under the apple boughs/ about the lilting house and happy/ as the grass was green.' Don't you remember?"

"I guess you used to sing it, but it's been a long time."

"I know, but it shows you what Earth was like. Don't you see? There was this little boy living on a farm, like in the tomten book, and he said, 'I had the trees and leaves trail with daisies and barley/ down the rivers of the windfall light."

"What does that mean?"

Alpha reached for the guitar and started strumming the chords. "'And as I was green and carefree,' anyway it shows you what an absolutely stupid, stupid, stupid idea it was to come here! 'Time let me play and be/ golden in the mercy of his means/ and green and golden I was huntsman and herdsman/ the calves sang to my horn/ the foxes on the hills barked clear and cold/ and the sabbath rang slowly in the pebbles of the holy streams.' Don't you remember? It makes me mad as hell that they robbed us of all that!"

"How mad is hell?"

"What?"

"You said mad as hell."

"This *is* hell! Don't you know that? Dad and Mom chose to come here, so they put us smack in the middle of hell." Alpha placed the guitar on the kitchen table, turned on his heel and left.

\+ + +

They had better days. Mom had begun teaching Alpha to play her guitar before she died, so sometimes he would strum and sing to Beta. But they were all Earth songs. Foolish children's songs. He strummed a chord and started singing:

All God's critters got a place in the choir,
Some sing low and some sing higher,
Some sing out loud from the telephone wire,
And some just clap their hands, or paws, or anything they got now.

He strummed the chord and picked out the tune for a bit. Beta loved it and joined him singing the second verse:

The dogs and the cats they take up the middle
Where the honey bee hums and the cricket fiddles
The donkey brays and the pony neighs,
And the old coyotee howls.

They both raised their heads and howled, hoping to imitate a sound Alpha had heard on the movie videos.

He stopped singing. Beta had, years ago, asked him to draw pictures of each of those animals, except for the donkey, because there was a donkey he could see in the Nativity Set. Alpha had tried. He didn't know what a cricket looked like; it ended up being a mouse playing a violin, and his version of a cat wouldn't have been recognized by anyone on Earth, but he had seen wolves in his mother's stories and she had said coyotes were a smaller version.

"I think a coyote looks a lot like a fox," he told Beta.

Beta smiled. "Let's sing it again," he said.

\+ + +

Alpha spent nine hours fixing the WR. He laid out all the manuals on the floor and took his time disassembling and reassembling the parts. He couldn't afford to make a mistake. Fortunately, he had stored ten gallons of water in the extra storage tank, which was the maximum the unit could reclaim from their waste and from the breathable air, so when the WR began to hum again, they still had nine gallons left, but it worried Alpha. He didn't relish dying of thirst. He spent an extra hour that night with the binoculars scanning the dark, glittering skies. He even found himself saying, "Come on, tomten, why don't you help us out."

When he finally walked out of Communications and down the corridor, he saw that Beta, wrapped in a blanket, had fallen asleep in the chair in the living room. He didn't bother to wake him.

\+ + +

When he climbed the ladder in the morning, Beta was talking to the light outside.

"Would you give that up?" Alpha shouted down the corridor. "I don't need a helper who is insane!"

The skinny little boy looked over at him with his big brown eyes, got up, folded his blanket, and said, "I'll make breakfast. You need to go push the dead button."

Alpha glared at him, turned, and headed toward Communications. The sun was high. The AC unit was working hard. He could hear the hum, and a squeaking had begun in the one big fan two days ago. The huge suction and fan system was located beneath Communications in Engineering, accessed by a stairway. He decided he'd have to go back down there and open up the vent and find out what was wrong, but after breakfast, Beta found a loose connection on the far side of the living room, so he had to pull out the adhesives and clamps to tighten it up. It made him angry since he knew that he'd put off fixing the fan for too long already and now that he'd made up his mind to fix it, this was an added delay.

After handing Alpha the adhesive tube, Beta said, "Things are going to be all right."

Alpha unscrewed the tube lid and glanced at his brother. "What?"

"I don't know, but I've been asking for help and I think things are going to be all right if we are patient."

Alpha tried to hold his temper as he squeezed in the glue and tightened the clamps. As soon as the clamps were firm, he turned on Beta. "Why would a tomten talk to you, you crazy little squirt! Why would an angel talk to a dumb little brother when the commander's right here?"

"He doesn't talk to me, but I've been asking for help and now I don't feel worried anymore."

"Well, great for you. But I am worried and I'm going to stay worried."

"What good does that do?"

"It keeps me alert and thinking. That's all we've got, so we better use it."

"Maybe. But I think we need some outside help. And maybe there is a tomten or an angel or something."

"I don't need an insane brother."

"Was Mom insane?"

Alpha said nothing.

Toward sundown of their 24-and-a-half-hour day, he had the panels fixed. Beta had been drawing pictures of Alpha and himself climbing a tall orchid tree but was now in the chair talking to the dying light as Alpha walked by on his way to put the last of the tools away. He walked over to Beta. "So, what's Angel Tomten got on his mind now?"

Beta stared out at the violet dust clouds fifty miles away across the barren plain. The sun had dropped below the ridgeline behind them leaving the ridge in dark silhouette, but far to the east the last light was turning distant dust clouds mauve and violet and pink.

Beta didn't answer, but he said he wasn't too worried anymore.

Alpha laughed. "Well maybe old Tomten's got your messages."

They made their way to Communications.

"It's late," said Beta. "Maybe we should go to bed and work on the fan tomorrow."

"Sit around and wait? What have we been doing for six years? Beta! I'm structured mentally and physically to run this place and you are going to help me do it."

"Let's go to bed," Beta said. "We need outside help."

"You're bat-shit crazy!"

"What is a bat . . . and why is its shit crazy?"

"Forget it. That's just something Dad used to say. Let's get to work."

"You're tired and I'm tired. Let's sleep and then work."

Alpha pulled the wheezing door open, closed it after Beta walked through, and automatically punched the Reporting Button as he walked past. The green light appeared as always and the dark screen, as always, stared back at him. They walked over to the round window. The dried space suits beyond were flapping in a hard wind, exposing a long shank of his father's leg bone. He remembered that first helpless week after the explosion when all he could think to do was sob and yell.

"I don't think we should do this," Beta said.

"I think we *should* do this," said Alpha.

"You're tired, Alpha. It's easy to make mistakes when you're tired. You tell me that all the time."

"Well, next time you see old Tomten, tell him I've got to take care of my responsibilities and my brother needs to obey me."

They climbed the ladder down into the Engineering Unit. While his little brother stood behind him, Alpha removed the cover panel from the suction system. He had, of course, shut the system down. It was an essential piece of equipment because it recirculated all the air in the entire habitat several times a day while an attached machine extracted the necessary percentage of water from the air and returned it to the water recycler. The engineering room was crowded with airtight vents, sealed machinery, and electrical cables. One insulated tank carried hydrazine, a very toxic jet fuel from which nitrogen was extracted and the remaining hydrogen molecules were combined with oxygen in the Combination System to provide added water for the habitat as the remaining nitrogen was funneled into a fertilizer tank for the now demolished farming system.

There wasn't much room to maneuver in the compartment, so Alpha was careful when he handed a panel to Beta, who took it up the stairs into

Communications and stood it against a wall, then climbed back down. To get to the squeaking fan, Alpha was using an electric drill with a screwdriver bit. He removed a second panel.

Beta took it upstairs and returned.

It seemed almost inevitable that Alpha would take that next screw out. It held a one-inch- diameter stainless steel cylinder, a section of piping that ran directly in front of the fan. It seemed the obvious next step, but he was tired and failed to read the manual's next step. As soon as Alpha squeezed the trigger of the drill and the screw loosened, a fine sharp spray of pressurized hydrazine shot across the room into Beta's face, blinding him. Beta opened his mouth to scream as he jerked back his head which allowed the pressurized stream access into his open mouth. The boy slammed his head into the metal door jamb which mercifully knocked him out as he inhaled the hydrazine and soon choked to death.

Alpha, whose father had trained him well, managed to click the button on the electric screw gun so that he could reverse the motion and tighten the screw as his brother fell. As the screw tightened, the spray fanned across Alpha's forehead, beginning to scorch his skin. He managed to keep pressure on the screw until it tightened and stopped the spray, but already he could feel the skin on his scalp and forehead beginning to burn. He dropped the drill, ripped off his own t-shirt, wiped his forehead and eyes, then began wiping Beta's face. He began crying out his brother's name over and over and over.

He ran up the stairs with his crumpled up t-shirt to the WR where he soaked it in water and ran it back to Beta to wipe the hydrazine from his brother's face, but there was nothing he could do. Beta had stopped breathing and that was that. He sat back stunned. He wiped his own forehead again with the soaked shirt, but the burning sensation increased.

He held his brother in his arms and lost track of time.

\+ + +

Alpha awoke. His brother's body had stiffened. He laid it down and howled. He rose, climbed the stairs, and staggered through Communications, out the wheezing door, and down the corridor howling and sobbing and howling again. By the time he made his way to the kitchen and soaped his head and scalp, there was a deep burn on his forehead and he clenched his teeth as he put his head under the faucet and ran water to clean off the soap.

He stumbled around the living area, through the kitchen, and back down the corridor, crying out, slamming his head into the hard plastique making his burnt forehead bleed, then stumbled on.

\+ \+ \+

The next night he sat in the old worn-out chair in Communications, staring at the console and its one green light. He couldn't bring himself to look out the round side-window because that afternoon he had dressed himself in one of the remaining space suits, dressed Beta in another one, and had dragged his brother's skinny body out the airlock and had laid it on top of the bones of his parents. He felt that he needed to do something by way of a funeral service, but he had never attended one.

He recalled an old movie he had watched with his mother in which a boy who has already lost his father, attends the funeral of his mother. Black-clothed men and women walk through a desolate Russian landscape in late fall as strange, haunting music accompanies the procession. The boy following the casket bearers looks up at the falling, wind-blown leaves of a nearby grove of trees as the haunting music, some kind of Russian chant accompanied by a stringed instrument something like a guitar, intensifies and reaches a kind of crescendo. But on Mars: no falling leaves. No trees at all.

After laying his little brother down on the ripped suits and bones of his parents, he had considered walking away from the shelter, climbing over the ridge and away, walking and walking till his oxygen supply ran out, but in the end he found himself screaming at himself for failing to read that one necessary line in the manual that warned not to loosen the fatal screw of the hydrazine piping.

After laying his brother to rest, he had returned through the double airlock, taken off his space suit, and walked to Communications. His forehead and scalp wound had clotted, and the burning sensation was intense, but he didn't bother to bandage it.

Now he sat staring at the console and its one green light.

He could still hear the regular squeaking of the fan that he had failed to fix. He had replaced the two panels and screwed them tight and flipped on the breaker and the air conditioning unit had returned to service. Life had its requirements.

Eventually he looked up through the clear dome at the moonless sky. Somewhere out there he noticed a brief flash of fire. He stared at it.

It disappeared. He picked up the binoculars and trained them on that star-speckled section of sky. The flash reappeared. He could see it clearly. The supply ship.

+ + +

The old man stood ankle deep in the clear, running water of a stream that eased over sand and limestone pebbles beneath the deep shadows of oaks and walnuts and a tall, white-trunked sycamore tree whose heavy roots had been partially undercut by the running stream. Gazing up, he noticed that the large, yellow-green leaves of the upper limbs of the sycamore were catching the evening sun.

He waded into deeper, shadowed, jade-green, sun-dappled water and felt the current gently swirling around his shins. Even after 60 years on Earth, he was still mesmerized by running water, its clean swirling and dipping and turning, the change in color from deep green to sky-reflecting blue, to the transparent revelation of stones and a swaying deep-green moss in the current, all in the space of several feet. Several black water bugs circled and swerved like tiny bumper cars at a fair while delicate water striders fled his presence on thin insect legs that dimpled the surface.

The summer afternoon was hot and the water cool. He remembered bringing his two sons here when they were five and six years old. A plate-sized snapping turtle had slid into dark dead leaves at the bottom of the clear stream. To impress the boys, he had reached down and grabbed the exposed tail of the big turtle and pulled it dripping out of the water. The boys had gasped and shouted; its blunt nose, clawed feet, plated armor looked to them like a dinosaur. They had found a small stick from the bank and the older boy had held the half-inch-thick twig near the head of the turtle. The turtle had hissed and Alpha had smelled fish on its breath. Then, in a flash, the turtle snapped at the twig and broke it in two. Alpha's hand had slipped and the heavy turtle had splashed into the stream. They had watched it dive into the deeper current and disappear.

Now, he turned and sloshed his way to shore and climbed the bank, making his way up a forest path in his soaked boots to the open meadow. He walked to a wicker chair placed beneath a leafy hackberry tree, part of the small forest that lined the quiet, meandering stream. He sat down.

The hot summer afternoon was lazily falling asleep. The heavy heat lay like a soft, lucent blanket. He settled back into the wicker chair and breathed in deeply.

Far off to the west a thunderhead rose above wooded hills, obscuring the sun. The rimlit borders of the cloud were a bright silver, but the dark interior kept erupting: bright white, yellow, and peach-colored flashes every few seconds. He reached down and unlaced his wet boots, extracted his feet, and pulled off the soaked socks, wringing them out and draping them on a nearby branch. He settled back into the chair, flexed his toes, and closed his eyes.

A few minutes later, a harsh, rasping sound woke him. On a long, arched stem of seeded grass, a pale green grasshopper bobbed in a sudden breeze. A katydid. Its sharp, almost painfully loud call carried over the meadow before him like the amplified sound of a steel file drawn across metal. He watched the insect's long, threadlike antennae move about. From the far side of the meadow there was an answering rasping call.

He watched the katydid. Not long, he thought, till the little spread-toed tree frogs would open their mouths and enter the evening chorus.

He heard a faint rumble of thunder and glanced west again. The storm cloud was building high into the evening air, drifting now above the gold orb of the setting sun. A nearby cloud of gnats caught a ray of light as they rose and fell in the still, humid air.

He stretched his bare feet and closed his eyes again, pulling his hat down over his eyes, wondering if the thundercloud would drift north or catch him here. If it came, he intended to stay and let it soak him down.

Now he heard a distant squeak behind him, beyond the little stream. Someone was opening the lower windows of the monastery's tall, stone chapel, built in a clearing beyond the stream. It was hot and the monks would need the windows opened for their vesper songs.

He looked out across the meadow, out beyond the line of squat hedge-apple trees to a ripened field of perennial wheat he had developed years before. Working with the Land Institute of Research in Salina, Kansas, he had, over the last four decades, helped develop a series of perennial grains to replace traditional wheats and sorghums so that farmers no longer needed to plow up fields and replant every year. Fifty years ago, he had taken to agronomy and attended Kansas State University, the school that had trained his mother. By crossbreeding sorghums or wheat with native grasses, farmers no longer needed to plow and replant their fields; the perennial grains reappeared each spring. For two decades, he had traveled the Earth promoting this technology that saved farmers work and fuels and prevented the loss of billions of tons annually of blown away top soils.

Now he looked down and watched a black cricket move past his toes and disappear into grass-clothed shadows. The thick and tangled grasses of unkempt pasture now fringed in late sunlight were full of life.

He took another deep breath. The low sun's rays silhouetted a large spider hung from a delicate web stretched tightly from a low hanging hackberry limb. She was working meticulously, connecting the transparent silk webbing, leaving rectangular interstices. He watched it, marveling again at the shining lace she hung upon, she the seamstress of a shining window opening toward the setting sun.

A heavy, breathless evening. No wind. The katydid had flown, and he could just hear the rush and trickle of the little stream behind him purling through pebbles and rocks.

'Now as I was green and golden,' the words trailed through his mind . . . 'and happy as the day was long . . .'

Someone was approaching, splashing through the stream behind him and ascending the footpath. Alpha thumbed up his hat brim and looked back.

The young man in his black robe carried a broken limb in one hand.

"What you doing with a stick, Brother Gilbert? Going to rap me on the head to wake me up?"

The young man smiled. "I hate the spiders this time of year. Those big fat ones that hang across the paths. They give me the creeps! So I whack my way along the path to keep them out of my face."

Alpha smiled and nodded.

"You coming to Vespers this evening, Doc?"

"No, Brother Gil. You've opened the windows. I'll hear you singing."

The young man smiled, nodded, and returned through forest shadows. The monks of the monastery had long used his perennial wheats and sorghum grains, had helped him do the laborious work each spring of cross pollinations, and now were growing and harvesting enough each year to feed themselves and make their donations to the city food bank.

To his left, the eastern sky beyond another line of small, wooded hills was cloudless. If the rain held off, he would stay in his wicker chair to watch the stars appear.

Later, Mars would rise beyond those eastern hills and he would spend some time talking to his brother.

The Current

Two young men in a small boat were floating down the broad back of the Volga River some miles south of Kazan in the Soviet Union. The year was 1939, and the late summer sun shone through a high film of cloud over the long, meandering river, over its levees and low, forested hills, its wide meadows and reedy marshes. One boy, dark-haired and stocky, pulled easily at the oars of the little rowboat while facing his fair-haired, studious friend who was sitting in the boat's stern flipping through a handful of note cards, glancing away as he sought a word or a date, then flipping the card over to confirm his answer.

All around them the great brown river was moving—roiling up from the depths, lifting and mixing the silts from plowed farmlands with the raw sewage of the little villages and, from farther upstream, the run-off of chemical and industrial plants, refineries and rock quarries—lifting and carrying the two young men too, each of them twenty years old, schoolmates from Rostov on the Don in their little, wobbly rowboat.

"Koka! Think of it," said the blond boy with the cards. "Just three weeks and we'll take the train to Moscow, to the most prestigious program in the country. Come get me, Moscow Institute of Philosophy, Literature and History!" He sat back and laughed, singing the long name again to the far bank.

His friend smiled and kept pulling at the oars.

"Koka! Now, at this time, in this place, at the apex of historical advancement!"

Koka smiled again. "Apex of historical advancement," he said. "Sounds like a phrase from Professor Solyinka. Did you write down absolutely everything that madman said?"

"Madman? You don't like him because he made you work!"

"Who's doing the work now, Sasha?" Koka leaned back into the oars, shook his black hair out of his eyes and said, "Apexes of historical advancement are beyond me. For all we know, we're sliding into chaos."

The current was breaking into choppy little waves as a brisk breeze swept down from a forested highland behind them. The wooden boat swayed with the slap of the waves. "You see?" Sasha laughed, putting down his cards and leaning back in the stern, "Even the wind is with us, pushing us on. And look there!" He sat up. "A village. Over there, beyond the bend. We'll pull over there and replenish our supply of potatoes. And maybe some sausage. We can afford a little sausage can't we?"

"I could eat sausage, Sasha," said Koka, turning to look behind him. "Hard biscuits and scrawny apples now for two days. We need meat, fresh bread, potatoes. This little trip through Solyinka's 'great heartland of the nation' can empty a man's belly."

They were silent for a time. No sound but the regular creaking of the oars in the wooden oarlocks and the slight slash of the dipping oars. The little boat rolled along with the following waves and the cool breeze counteracted the work of the high sun.

Rounding a headland, they saw a motorized launch chugging upriver, its diesel engine kicking black smoke into the wind. The long steel hull was stacked with crates of live chickens: black hens, speckled ones, browns, reds, whites, greys—all stuffed in their wooden crates, feathered heads poking out absurdly through the slats, cramped wing feathers and tail feathers ruffling in the breeze.

"Chicken soup for the cooking pots of Kazan," said Koka.

"Or maybe on to Moscow," said Sasha.

"I wish they'd let us have one. Roasted chicken. How long has it been since we ate chicken, Sasha. I haven't seen a chicken for two days."

Three boys in ragged shirts sat on the stack of chicken crates and waved as the launch rumbled by. Koka nodded to them and kept a rhythm with his rowing. He was naked to the waste and in the last two weeks his strong, young body had browned in the sun. He was shorter than his companion, and his muscles moved smoothly beneath the skin. Sasha was thinner, with great, wondering eyes that darted constantly from the cards to the tree-lined shore of the wide river, then back to the near bank where men and women of a collective farm were picking apples in a small meadow near shore, their wooden ladders thrust up into the branches. The men wore loose peasant pants and caps, the women were in long skirts, their scarves tied tightly around their hair.

"Don't you ever stop studying, Sasha?"

"We have time, Koka. The boat moves slowly. I can take in the sights and pick up a few lines from Pushkin at the same time."

"You're saying I row too slowly?"

Sasha looked up. "The great Volga moves slowly. It has to carry a lot of history on its back; it can't hurry. You know, even Vikings used to run their longboats down the Volga to the Caspian Sea, carrying gold and furs and beautiful slave girls."

"Ah, beautiful slave girls. Things weren't so bad back then."

"Unless you were a slave girl," Sasha said. "The poor and weak have always been oppressed, Koka. Now, in our own time, at last, the workers have the power to shape their own affairs."

"The serfs were released last century, Sasha. We haven't practiced slavery for a long time."

"Wake up, Koka! The serfs were still under the boots of the land owners! Still oppressed. Now, at long last, the workers are free to own the means of production. You and I, though born of poor people get to go to university."

Reedy marshes past the headland marked the entry of a nearby stream while the far bank held a forest of pine and fir rising into dark hills. Past the nearby apple orchard, a field of wheat stubble spread over a nearby ridge. Far across the water, they could hear a woodcutter's axe chopping, chopping.

"History is moving us, Koka. We are in the center of everything. Look at the fields over there. Enough wheat to feed a world and a movement."

"Then why could we buy nothing but apples in that last village? No wheat. Not even potatoes."

"Don't know. I'm not a farmer, Koka. These country people haven't caught on yet to the currents of change. But they will. Progress is ours, Koka; change is inevitable. We've got science and technology. Never before have we had such opportunity to change the world."

Koka stopped rowing and let the boat rock along in the current. "You wanted to come on this trip, to see the great heartland of our country,

Sasha. Well this is it: little towns and villages, little places, little people. But you keep reaching way out there to mass movements, to global fronts, internationalism, to vast, classless societies. You want to blend everything together in one big soup. I like my potatoes mashed with cream and butter, my cabbage boiled with a little vinegar, roast beef in gravy with melon pickles on the side and horseradish."

"But Koka, don't you want to stir things up? Ignite the fires." Sasha's face turned to the high sun, his long, blonde hair catching the breeze. "What's an education for, Koka? Believe me, even the reactionary peasants will listen in time. They don't like the collective farms, but this will lead to great efficiencies. Change is coming, Koka. And I want to be there carrying the torch."

"Carrying the torch! I hate those cliches: 'the dawn of the future, building a new world.' Life is lived in the particulars, Sasha. A single flower. A bright day. Wasn't that the way Pushkin had it? Habitual, everyday things. These hands on these oars. 'A pot of soup, and my fine self.'

"More, Koka. Such a vast country we live in! From the Baltic Sea to the Pacific, from the Pole to the Black Sea. And the movement will spread beyond that. Spring winds are blowing."

"And how is your little novel coming along, my friend?"

"You know very well it will not be a small book."

"Oh yes, yes. What's the name of it?" He leaned back into his oars. "*The Meaning of the Cosmos*, or something?"

"A funny man. It's *The Meaning of the Twentieth Century* and you know it."

"Ah yes. Right. You've bitten off a smallish chunk, just a single century and less than half of it now past us."

"And why not? You know what The Revolution means for the world."

"I'm not so sure anymore, Sasha. The ideologies keep shifting. The National Economic Program was a failure: the speculators getting rich, the city people poorer. Now collectivization is all the rage . . . but speaking of revolutions, Sasha. What about Natasha? Anything I should know about that? All those walks in the moonlight. All those piano sonatas played on her parents' piano. Something's in the air and you're not telling me. Some kind of torch burning there."

"And why should I tell you?"

"Because we're friends, you little mouse. Friends talk."

Sasha settled back in the stern and closed his eyes, letting his free hand trail in the water. "I don't know, Koka. I spoke to her of love not long ago. We were sitting on a park bench in Rostov's Theatrical Park—you know the place. Well, I did tell her how utterly and completely I was in love with her. . ."

"And?"

Sasha opened his eyes and looked into the sky. "She cried."

"Tears? She wept?"

"Yes. What do you make of that?"

Koka kept rowing, glancing back from time to time to make sure of his direction. "She didn't explain?"

"No. But then I'm not the easiest person to love."

"True, Sasha. I'm surprised your own mother can put up with you. Your head is so full of politics and philosophy and literature. Studying all the time, writing."

"But that's what I am. Mother knows that and Natasha needs to know it too. Sometimes I think the trivia of married life will slow me down. And children. Who has time for children? We have so much to accomplish."

The brown little waves bumped against the hull of the old wooden boat as Koka turned slowly round the bend. As they moved behind a tree line, the breeze calmed, and the river grew still, mirroring the tall fir trees along the east bank. Koka stroked the boat toward the poles and weathered planking of a little country dock.

A scattering of log huts stood here and there, others staggered up the slope behind the dock. Steep, sway-backed roofs bent beneath grey wooden shingles weathered by time. Stiff old oak trees, their leaves already brown, cast pools of shade here and there in the warm afternoon sunlight. A single goat grazed behind a stick fence and a small chicken and a few yellow chicks pecked about in the dirt. Beyond a stand of fir trees stood a short, onion-turreted church.

They saw the figure of a fisherman sitting on the dock stringing new wooden blocks along the top rope of his net. The net lay tangled along the grey planks of the walkway. They could see him squint up from time to time as the two boys approached in their rowboat.

"Where are we?" called Sasha.

The man looked up and gazed at the boys as they drifted near. "The Union of Soviet Socialist Republics," he said.

The boys looked at each other. "What's the name of this place?"

"We call it Krasnoya Glinka, but there's hardly enough here now to hold a name."

"Can we buy potatoes here? Maybe some sausage?" Koka asked.

The man grinned, coughed, and spat. "Caviar. Only caviar." He watched them as they looped a rope over a post and climbed from their boat. His face was brown like the river with a tangle of creases like his net. His hands never stopped working the drying net. Little bits of broken fish scales sparkled here and there in the brown netting and the whole tangle smelled of fish and river.

Koka pulled on his shirt and said, "But we can't afford caviar. We just need some potatoes or biscuits."

"Caviar up there in the canning factory." The man jabbed a thumb over his shoulder.

Sasha buttoned his shirt and pulled on a sweater. "But it's September, the harvests are in, or coming in. Somebody will sell us some food."

The man looked away as he kept plucking the knots apart with a little wire tool, sliding the wooden floats along the braided hemp, then retying the knots with a quick jerk of his hand.

They stepped over his net and walked off the planking and up the hill through the dust. They were hungry, but there seemed to be no one around. A dog lifted its head from beneath a shrub, thumped its tale once, and again rested its muzzle on its paws. Here, out of the wind, the sun was strong.

Making their way up the rutted dirt road, they found several men and women sitting outside the church eating. They were eating apples, though the place smelled strongly of fish. The wooden church building's white paint was peeling; the wooden onion dome still held a cross, but the green copper sheathing around it had split in places and the wood beneath it was open to the weather so the turret sagged a bit to one side.

Walking up to the church, Koka asked for potatoes or biscuits. One of the men motioned them inside. A little loudspeaker nailed above the door was blaring out the usual radio messages about valiant workers forging the steel of a new generation. They passed through the open door of the church into a little room lined with shelves. A man sat behind a desk, his chair propped on two legs against the wall, his long legs and cheap felt boots resting on the desk. His hair was cut short but a big moustache drooped over either side of his wide mouth. He took a cigarette from his lips and nodded a greeting. Koka asked for potatoes or biscuits.

"You have rubles?"

Koka nodded and asked how much.

The man shrugged and stated a figure.

"That much for potatoes and biscuits?" Koka asked.

The man reached under his desk without removing his boots from the table and pulled out a small burlap sack and set it on the desk. After considerable haggling, they settled on a price for six wrinkled potatoes. The shelves behind the man contained a few scattered cans, some small sacks. On the floor was a basket of apples.

"Biscuit flour?" Koka asked.

The man let his old boots drop to the floor, replaced the cigarette in his mouth, and pushed himself to his feet. He reached for a sack and placed it on a scale.

While dark-haired Koka pulled the money from his pocket, Sasha stood in the doorway that led to the old sanctuary. Four long wooden tables slick with the blood and slime of the fish filled the area. A cat was crouching in a window wolfing down fish entrails. A large, wooden bucket near the door held three sturgeon heads, one of them as big as a boot. Next to a machine fastened to a table at the far end, was a small stack of sealed cans. In a slant of sunlight a dusty, painted icon of a tall, thin saint in faded robes stared solemnly at the caviar.

Koka asked for sausage. The man sat down and laughed, a low, rasping laugh. He took a long drag on his cigarette, sucking the burning nub right up under his moustache, then flicked it into the dust and exhaled a cloud of smoke. "You want sausage, go back to the university, boys." He leaned back in the wooden chair and appraised them.

"The collective farms here don't raise pigs?" Koka asked.

"Oh yes. Pigs, cows, horses, chickens, ducks."

"Why no sausages, then?"

"What are you, inspectors?" The man glanced over at Sasha standing in the doorway.

"Of course not," Koka said. "We're just students on vacation. We just want to eat."

The man sat back in his chair and lifted his boots again to the table top. He looked at them both. "Maybe our young students should know this. Last winter, we ate glue."

The boys looked at the man.

"Last winter, children, before the Feast of the Magi, my wife boils our horse's harness for three days and then we eat it with the last of the horse-hoof glue. Horse-sweat soup, we call it. The old, broken mare herself had decided to avoid the difficulties of another Soviet winter, and visited our collective stomachs before the Nativity. Don't talk to me of sausage."

"But why is this happening?"

"So you young intellectuals can eat, I suppose."

"Can you sell us fish?"

"We have a contract with the state. We cannot sell fish to locals."

"How about a couple of fish heads to boil with our potatoes?"

"That's our own supper tonight. No fish for sale."

+ + +

They walked back down to the dock eating apples.

"Good fresh apples," murmured Sasha.

"Let's cook some up with biscuits tonight," said Koka.

Sasha nodded.

As they followed the rutted dirt road down to the dock, the dog got up and walked over to sniff their bag of supplies, but soon turned back to the shade of the bush.

The fisherman was still there. His weathered hands kept untying knots on his net, threading the wooden blocks, and retying.

"Want an apple?" asked Sasha, reaching into the sack he was carrying.

The man looked up. "No caviar?" He held up his hand and caught the russet-speckled apple Sasha tossed him. The man bit into it.

"Any fish for sale?" asked Koka.

The man looked away across the river, his stubble jaws working the apple. "Where you from?"

Both boys said at once, "Rostov."

"A long way from home. What are you looking for?"

"We're students," Sasha said, as he stepped over the net and dropped his sack of apples in the boat. "We just wanted to see something of the mother country before going to Moscow to school."

"Moscow," the man said, tearing a bite out of the apple.

Koka followed Sasha, stepping down into the boat, and dropped his small sack of flour and the little bag of six potatoes and looked again at the fisherman. "No fish to sell at all?"

"You have anything to trade?"

"Yes, absolutely. Rubles."

The man looked at his apple and sucked at the core, nibbling around the seeds. "Two small lesch, boys. Too small for the fish contracts, you understand."

"Yes. Yes," said Koka. "How much?"

They settled on a price and Sasha counted out the kopeks and handed the man the coins. The man scooted back on the planking and leaned over the water, reached beneath the surface and pulled up a rope attached to a wire basket that held five or six bream. He selected the two smallest and tossed them into the boat where they flipped a time or two then lay still, their gills opening and closing.

+ + +

By evening they had rowed and floated another twenty miles.

Four horses stood on a spit of gravel watching them in the declining sun. Once they heard a woman and her daughter singing as they washed their clothes on the riverbank. The slow, sad melody followed them down the current. They floated by islands, the current twisting one way then another. Sasha was rowing now and Koka was flipping the cards, quizzing his friend on the details of dialectical materialism, on Hegelian principles of thesis, antithesis, synthesis, and after a few minutes of this, reading him an article from *Pravda*.

At length Koka rolled up the paper and pulled on a shirt and sweater. "It's getting cold. That north wind isn't letting up. We'll have frost by morning. So what do you think, Sasha? Why do the peasants eat glue?"

"I've been thinking about that. The communes are inefficient now. But they'll learn. Every revolution demands sacrifices, Koka."

"Yes, yes. Must break a few eggs, as they always say, to make an omelet. But there don't seem to be many eggs left around here."

Sasha's skinny arms pulled at the oars. "No revolution is perfect, Koka."

The great river carried them on, weaving between islands that cast long shadows over the rippling current. The sun was going down red-gold beyond a dark line of fir trees. Behind the banks to the east they could see grassy hills braided with orchards standing bright in the evening sun. Occasional barges, pushed by growling tugboats, moved upriver or down sending out wakes that rocked their little boat sharply back and forth.

By evening they had found a grassy bank on which to build a fire to boil their fish, potatoes and apples, and mix the dough for biscuits.

+ + +

At dawn Sasha sat up in the boat. He was shivering. He wrapped his thin arms around his ribs beneath his blanket and laughed, kicking at the sleeping bundle beside him. Koka's long body lay partly beneath the thwart where one of them would sit while the other rowed. "Koka! Wake up. Look at the frost. You were right!" He shook his blanket and a cloud of hoarfrost jumped sparkling into the grey light.

Koka's dark head appeared from under his blankets just as the frost crystals showered his cheek and he ducked back beneath his blankets.

Sasha struggled to sit up in the bottom of the boat, pulling the blanket around his thin shoulders and looked out onto the river. A heavy grey mist was rising from the water into the cold air above, obscuring the entire river, dissolving the near bank into a dark soup. The seats and gunwales of their boat were needled white with frost. The fog moved over and around them, drifting silently, folding and unfolding, taking on muffled shapes, moving slowly south, sometimes forming into drifting figures that looked to him like obscure groups of people: hunched old men in trailing coats, shawled women moving down a long, long road.

"Come on Koka, strip! I'm jumping in!" Sasha threw his blanket off, peeled his shirt over his head and pulled off his trousers. He stepped naked and barefoot onto the slippery plank at the stern, stooping to steady himself with a hand on the frosted gunwale, then stood slowly up, poised and ready. Through the drifting mist, a pale sun had risen like a flat white plate beyond the far bank, but he could not begin to see the distant bank. He looked back at his friend, a shadowy lump of woolen blankets lying on the floor of their boat. "Koka! It's a glorious morning. Sprout, you shriveled potato!"

He was about to leap when he saw, winging upriver, above the mist, a broken line of white pelicans. He gripped his ribs and watched them. There, beyond the fog, he counted almost fifty pelicans soaring into a brightening sky, stroking rhythmically through the air, forming and re-forming into lines, the morning sun struck them perfectly white against the high, blue sky.

"Koka, look," he said in a whisper, his dark eyes wide, his thin body swaying with the gentle rocking of the boat, his arms still clasping his ribs.

Koka's dark hair reappeared from beneath the blankets. He sat up and followed his friend's eyes.

"Birds. A bunch of white birds. This is what you get me up for?"

"Where are they going, Koka?" Sasha's eyes were fixed on the passing flock.

"Anywhere they like, I suppose."

"Anywhere," he breathed as the white birds passed southwards along the river and faded into the mist.

"But this is what you woke me for? Birds?" said Koka, lying back down and pulling the blanket over his head.

"No, this!" said Sasha and leaped, splashing down beside the boat.

Koka shouted as the cold slosh slapped over the gunwale, splashing his blankets. He sat up and grabbed the seat to steady himself, then began jerking off his shirt and pants as Sasha surfaced, shouting and laughing, "Cold, too cold for you, you fat river rat!"

Koka crouched naked on his blankets and stared at the slate-grey water.

"Jump! The water's warmer than the air! "

"This rat has a thin hide."

"Come on, Koka, I'm swimming out."

Koka swung over the side and dropped into the cold shock.

The two young men swam strongly into the current, but soon saw themselves carried beyond their little boat and out into the heavy mist. Losing their sense of direction, they turned this way and that, treading water. All about them the mist rose like thick smoke; they could no longer see the bank.

Sasha leaned back into the water and peered up through the fog, his white feet and legs floating to the surface as the current carried them on. "Which way, Koka?"

"Come on you mathematician, you should know your geometry. Swim at right angles to the current and we'll reach shore. Let's go, I'm starved." Swimming hard in the current, no longer feeling the cold, they turned for what they thought was shore.

Sasha could see Koka's dark wet hair bobbing through the fog several feet away and followed him with a breast stroke to keep him in sight.

On they swam, but the shrouded headland beyond them had turned a good deal of the Volga River back upon itself into a vast whirling eddy, sweeping them along in a great circle through the fog. Eventually they lost sight of each other and began calling to keep track of each other. Soon, because of the turning, chaotic current, they were swimming in different directions. Weary with the effort, they stopped calling. Drifting, listening, drifting, and swimming again, they kept moving toward what they thought was shore.

—Loosely based on a journey taken by Alexander Solzhenitsyn and a friend when they were 20 years old.

Narthex

The wind was running that afternoon, high, unhindered over hills and groves, level fields, and wooded valleys, thrashing the trees, chasing before it the heavy summer haze of previous weeks.

"There's change in the air," murmured Pastor Ezra Bradford as he stood gazing out the tinted glass doors of the large suburban shopping mall. Change in the air. It was another of the little clichés that used to so irritate his good wife. He smiled as the slow, sad memory caught him again. And now she had passed, and with her, so much of his energy and hopes and plans had evaporated.

The long afternoon idled by, made longer by that slight irritation of anxiety that always nagged him on days like this. He planned to be early for his appointment. He always arrived an hour or two early when appearing before the selection committee of a church to which he was candidating to be their new minister. He would use the time to look over the grounds, inspect the church building and surmise some opinion of the general welfare of the congregation. In younger years, he had turned down churches after such inspections, calling the selection committee and telling them that he had chosen a new path and apologizing for the late notice. But now Ezra Bradford was 62 years old. Congregations these days shunned the competence and wisdom of age and preferred energetic young pastors who could appeal to their youth. Still, he considered himself a successful minister: congenial, administratively efficient, and above all, a fine speaker. People had generally liked him, especially when accompanied by his wife whose sympathetic ear and social graces had balanced his more reserved, scholarly temperament.

She had died late last year. Since then, he had grown pensive and distant. The constant rush of activities at the large, suburban church had wearied him. He found himself longing for a place of quiet retreat, time to rethink those values he had preached for so many, many years. He had found so little time to reflect, so little time to pray through all those busy, successful years.

After reading a notice about this small, older congregation whose minister had just retired, he had examined his pension and decided to at least go through with the interview.

The selection committee of this country church had set the appointment for Friday at three in the afternoon, so he had driven into the neighboring city, slept the night in a Holiday Inn Express, then stopped for lunch at this immense shopping center. Thirty-five years ago when he was fresh out of seminary, he and his wife had started a small church in just such a mall as this, taking over the space vacated by a failing toy store, then, as the congregation grew, they had moved into a larger section of the mall that had been abandoned by the Sears company. Six years later, they had built a larger brick and mortar establishment in the suburbs, a building that in many ways was a more dignified version of the shopping center: rectangular, flat-roofed, with an adjacent parking lot, even a welcoming coffee shop nestled near the glassed front doors. Since then he had served several churches, moving on when life grew stale or contention tore a congregation.

After eating lunch, he had strolled through the relatively empty mall. Somewhere, music floated in the background, remote and nondescript. He noticed that the entire building was almost vacant on this Friday afternoon. The great malls were dying, but the mall-like churches had been multiplying.

He looked at his watch. Two hours yet. He continued his stroll, taking another lap around the inside of the mall. Once a revival preacher had come to his parents' little country church when Ezra was seven or eight. The church, a split from a larger Baptist congregation, had been meeting in a relocated and refurbished army barracks. The revival preacher, scheduled for three nights, had stood before them, not shouting and raving like the tent revivalists of old, but quietly evoking scenes of another world. He was a frail, elderly man with a wisp of grey hair and penetrating blue eyes. He had stepped from behind the pulpit, holding the edge of the wooden podium with one thin hand while grasping a heavy, tattered Bible in the other hand.

Young Ezra had sat on the front row of metal folding chairs watching. Somehow the power of the man's quiet words had lifted the young boy and it had seemed to him that if the preacher were not anchored to that pulpit, he might float away on the current of his stories. The old man's eyes had gazed out over the heads of the hundred or so seated congregants, mostly Iowa farmers and small businessmen and their wives. As he told the story, the preacher seemed to be peering into that ancient land of dry mountains and hilltop citadels as a passing camel caravan was wending its way up and out of a far grove of palm trees shimmering in the heat. The camel men stopped on a desert ridge and looked into a rocky valley filled with a vast encampment of black goat-hair tents collected along a small winding stream. Herds of cattle, goats, and sheep grazed over the farther hills, but the camel men noticed a huge, rectangular tent surrounded by concentric rows of curtains where smoke rose from a stone altar as robed priests moved about the place.

The preacher looked down at his Bible and read of blue, and purple, and scarlet fabrics, of badgers' skins, of oil and spices, onyx stones and jewels. The preacher looked up and described the golden lampstand, the golden altar of incense. The boy's mind was carried into that scene, but then the preacher's voice stopped. Young Ezra had looked up. The man was leafing through the pages of his big black Bible. He lifted the book and read of a vast city floating down out of the sky, a city of transparent gold decorated with onyx, topaz, and names of jewels the boy could not pronounce.

To young Ezra it had seemed the old man could see the ranks of angels in festal array, the jasper-jeweled walls of this unimaginable city floating out of a dark sky, could see the huge foundation stones and tall gates, each carved of a single massive pearl . . . .

Now Ezra glanced at his watch. An hour and a half before the meeting. He pushed open the glass doors of the mall. The hot summer wind met him, whipping his suit and scattering his thinning hair. A few shoppers straggled ahead of him through the vast parking lot. He followed them, the dazzle of windshields catching him in succession as he hurried toward his Honda Civic.

\+ + +

Following a map the committee had sent him, he turned east, passing a block of new warehouses and several-story offices buildings brightly glassed.

A few minutes later, he rumbled over train tracks, driving along chain-linked fences, passing brick buildings with windows bricked shut, I-beams rusted in haphazard stacks near jumbles of fifty-five-gallon barrels. A concrete bridge took him over a littered drainage ditch into an older neighborhood of clapboard homes. He glanced with misgivings at homes succumbing to rental blight: houses parched for paint, weeds and bushes poking indiscriminately from under deteriorating porches, but soon the asphalt road turned to gravel and he was in the countryside.

He relaxed. Fields of wheat stubble alternated with the deep green of alfalfa fields fringed with yellowing summer grasses. The road turned north and passed between squat hedge trees on his right and the drying stalks of head-high corn to his left. Then he spotted a church steeple or tower of some sort. The church stood behind a white-trunked sycamore tree.

As he pulled into the parking lot on his left, he noticed a large plywood sign announcing Bethel Baptist Church. They had already painted over the name of the previous pastor. The limestone church rose into the late summer sky. It did not look like any Baptist church Ezra Bradford had ever seen. He supposed he had seen thousands upon thousands, ranging from makeshift storefronts to white-steepled New England churches, to metal warehouses, to massive brick fortresses. He stopped the car in the shade of the sycamore tree, opened his door, and stepped into the hot wind, trying to put on his flapping suitcoat. The dry cornfield across the road behind him shook and whispered in the wind.

It was not a large building, but he estimated it might hold 200 or more congregants. The yellowish stone walls and steeply pitched slate roof seemed a native part of an older, quieter land, but looking south along the road he had come, he could see faded hills backed by a rising thunderhead and a commotion of dark clouds. It looked like rain.

He glanced back at the church. "Old," he remarked, stating the obvious. He stood frowning up at the smooth stone gable that rose precipitously to a small tower topped not with a Baptist steeple, but with a stone Celtic cross. Next to the steep gable and attached to the north wall on his right stood a tall stone bell tower. Arched openings near the top were enclosed by sloped horizontal slats needing paint and backed by chicken wire to keep the pigeons, crows, and swallows out. He wondered if a bell still hung there.

He had never pastored a church with bells, but he liked them, had once been moved by the tones rolling out over the hot plains of La Mancha when he and his wife had vacationed in Spain.

Centered in the church's stone gable, he saw a round stained-glass window about four feet in diameter. A large piece of the window had been replaced by plywood and caulked shut. What remained was so begrimed by years of neglect that even the westering sun shining full upon it presented only a dull image of what appeared to be a madonna and child.

A sudden sadness passed through him as he stood there in the sun and the wind. He had never been one to grow sentimental over architecture. Buildings were utilitarian. If they were also beautiful, that was fine, but beauty was certainly decorative, not essential. But plywood?

A gust of blown dust from the gravel driveway caught his eyes. He reached in his suitcoat pocket for the small flashlight he always carried to these meetings so he could shine it into closets and bathrooms to get a feel for how well the place was cared for. On his left, south of the building, lay a church cemetery: a hundred gravestones stood here and there or leaned comfortably on thick patches of tall, uncut grasses. Beyond the graves, stood a line of oak trees rustling in the wind and behind them a pasture.

He turned to his right and walked north around the belltower. Rounding the stone tower, the church building sheltered him from the southwest winds. Seven tall lancet windows of stained glass divided the length of the sanctuary. Walking near, he could see dusty, haloed figures standing vigil in the windows. At the end of the sanctuary, a lower addition of the same yellow limestone intersected the church from the north, also roofed in the grey-green slate. A stone arch bisected this transept roofing a recessed door of oak. As he approached, he could see intricate traceries of stone winding up the legs of the arch, as if leafy vines had petrified. The church builders had spent serious money on decorations.

A rusted bicycle lay in the grass a few yards from the transept door.

He made his way around the entire building, finding another matching transept on the far side. Several ventilation pipes protruded from the roof, so he assumed the restrooms were there, and probably Sunday School classrooms. Walking around the southeast corner of the transept, the warm wind met him. He thought he should leave. Such a dilapidated place. The few members of this church clearly couldn't pay the bills. He glanced at his watch: 2:35, less than a half hour before his appointment. He stopped near the front steps and breathed in deeply of field and grove. He had lived in suburbs and cities for more than three decades, but he remembered the scents of that countryside church, the scents of youth.

He turned to look again at the distant rise of thunderclouds to the southwest. Several crows, cawing faintly, rode the south wind toward a distant line of cottonwood trees beyond the blowing cornfield.

He climbed the stone steps to the entryway. The double oak doors were embossed and riveted with ancient iron hinges. Two stone pillars anchored a gently pointed arch that framed the tall doors. Running his hands over the nearest pillar, he felt the weathered stone. In places cement had chipped out and fallen away.

He needed to leave before the committee arrived. He turned and walked down the steps toward his car, but turned for a last look. The midafternoon sun shone golden upon the native limestone as if the full power of that September sun were being absorbed within each cut stone, until stone by stone the whole face of the church emanated a mellow light. He looked at his car. The white branches of the tall sycamore tree that shaded his Honda swayed and the large green leaves flapped and rustled in the wind. The gravel parking lot shaded by trees reminded him again of his parents' old country church.

He still had a little time. He decided to see if the sanctuary was unlocked.

He hurried back to the wide stone steps and stepped up to the large double doors beneath the arch, noticing a small stone receptacle projecting from just inside the southern arch. Within, crumpled gum wrappers floated in a little brackish water.

The iron-hinged doors creaked and whined as he pulled them open.

He stepped inside. The interior swallowed up the day. He was standing in an arched narthex maybe ten feet wide and ten feet long. On either side wooden shelves and tables held brochures and pamphlets, a stack of church bulletins. He picked one up, folded it, and slid it into a pocket of his suit jacket. He moved toward a second set of doors; he pushed them open and stepped in. For a moment he thought he had interrupted a service in progress; the further oaken pews were full of soft, colored lights while the nearer pews were in deep shadow. He blinked. Of course the pews were empty. He saw that three windows on each side of the sanctuary had been painted over. Painted? Even for Ezra Bradford it seemed outlandish to paint over such carefully laid stained glass, an aesthetic desecration. He walked over to the first tall lancet window on his right and scratched at the whitish paint covering a man's robe, but could not scratch off the thick coating.

He turned to examine the sanctuary. All slept in shadowed stillness. The three painted windows on either side of the back half of the sanctuary cut off most of the light.

Beyond, up the central aisle, the fine, multicolored lights filtered through the remaining, unpainted stained-glass windows, especially on the south side where the sun shone more directly, illuminating the rows of amber pews. He glanced up. High above, heavy black ceiling beams crossed each other down the length of the sanctuary.

As he returned to the central aisle, he turned toward the front. Just then he heard behind him the sudden shutting of the front doors. He stopped and waited. The wind, he thought. Now the silence was complete. Walking slowly, his hands slid along the smoothness of the pews. He noticed the tops of the armrests had all been meticulously carved into oak leaves and acorns as if here, the old oaks still bore fruit.

At the front of the aisle stood a white table. Above it, a large, bulky pulpit interrupted the view. The white, stone table at the end of the aisle was beautifully carved in a bas-relief of vines and grapes with two robed figures at either end. He walked up to it and examined the two carved figures; one held a large, old-fashioned key, the other a sword: Peter and Paul, no doubt, standing in stone. How could a small, country church pay for such extravagance? They must once have had rich donors.

Moving around the table, he took three steps up to the chancel. Behind the pulpit were two rows of folding metal chairs, no doubt, for a small church choir. He looked up to the high eastern window. There, a haloed lamb shouldered a dusty, red pennant. Dropping his eyes down the stone wall, he expected to find a large cross, but there was nothing. . . but not quite nothing. As he stared at the wall, his eyes picked out five spaced holes in the smooth stone below the stained glass. Once there had been a cross.

He turned to face the back. Why hadn't he looked for a light switch? But, he decided, he liked the shadows, the stillness, the muffled sound of the wind outside. He turned to his left and walked along the front pew to the first lancet window on the north side. What he took to be four Biblical prophets were arranged around a central scroll that read, Sanctus, Sanctus, Sanctus. Each prophet, haloed in a faint golden light, gazed east toward the absent cross. One figure held a carpenter's saw, another a small tower, another a stone, and the last stood beside a ram. He was mystified.

He turned again and looked at the opposite windows across the sanctuary. The stronger southern light illumined a more familiar arrangement: around a jeweled book stood a winged man, an eagle, an ox, and a lion. A rich, jeweled border of reds, greens, and deep blues framed these symbols of the Gospel writers. The next southern window held a beardless saint holding a silver chalice from which an emerald serpent writhed. Ezra Bradford frowned at the strange image.

He turned and followed the northern aisle back to the windows that had been painted over. There the light ceased. Some of the paint was peeling. Small scrapings had fallen to the stone windowsill and he could make out the raised inscriptions: Augustine, Ambrose, Aquinas arranged around an IHS. The lead and glass left distinct impressions and enough paint had faded or fallen from Augustine that a pale green light shone through the figure's breast.

He moved to the next window. In each window stood a saint whose name he could only decipher like a blind man by feeling out the inscriptions. Some, he had never heard of: Jogues, Brebeuf, Lalemant, but most of the names were vaguely familiar to an evangelical minister. He understood why they had been painted over. These men had no place in an evangelical church.

As he turned again toward the entry, a light far up caught his eye. Over the entrance, he saw that first-seen window caulked and plywooded. The western sun shone full upon it, yet only a dim likeness of its original glory remained. A child was reaching for his mother's face, but the child's hand was gone, as was his mother's face, with only the points of a departed crown visible above the plywood. Had someone thrown a stone at the window? The mother's delicate hands held her son. A dusty golden light glimmered around the figures. Then, strangely, a half-forgotten children's rhyme began playing through his mind, and he whispered:

> The queen she sits upon the strand
> Fair as lily, white as wand;
> Seven billows on the sea,
> Horses riding fast and free,
> And bells beyond the sand.

Just as the verse passed his lips, the toll of a great bell shook the darkness. He stiffened and caught a nearby pew. Twice more the solemn bell rang, reverberating away into the stones.

"Three o'clock?" he asked out loud. He looked at his watch: 2:46. *Someone,* he thought, *has arrived and has rung the bell. Or maybe they have it set on a timer to ring out the hours and they're off by fourteen minutes.*

It seemed much darker now. No doubt the westering sun had passed behind a cloud. He stood listening. No voices. Somewhere he heard a door squeak and close. He was aware of a song, a thin, high voice singing some slow lament far away. He sat down in a pew.

Someone had rung the bell and was singing. Or could the brief song have come from the radio of a passing car, or maybe he had mistaken the wild moaning of the wind through the crack in the front door. Within the church, all was muffled, mute, obscure.

He turned in the pew and looked behind him. Above the narthex doors to the sanctuary he noticed some figures. He fumbled in his suitcoat pocket for the little flashlight, clicked it on and turned it to the figures above the doors. Painted, white-robed figures stood above the narthex doors, their almond eyes entranced, bound hands folded in prayer, austere faces pale in the sudden light seemed unaware of their own wounds bleeding crimson upon their white robes. Two young men, a woman and child, shot through with arrows.

Ezra clicked off the flashlight and frowned again. Strange to have such vivid visions of death placed where any child could see them.

He stood, and instinctively walked to the central aisle and turned toward that familiar bastion of intellectual security, the great, central pulpit. As he approached, he noticed that on the back wall, on either side of the absent cross, carved stone pedestals projected from recessed niches. He climbed the three steps to the chancel and flicked on his flashlight. What originally must have been statues had been replaced by banners. Bold banners with raucous letters and exclamation points proclaimed, "REJOICE !!" and on the opposite wall, colorful letters shouted "PEACE ON EARTH !!!"

He turned back down the stairs, forgetting the pulpit, turning the flashlight to his watch: 2:51. Strange that no one on the committee had arrived by this time. But who had rung the bell? Maybe they were gathering in the attached building with the arched doorway.

He hurried back down the aisle toward the entry. He passed beneath the enchanted martyrs, opened the doors to the narthex, and stepped quickly to the front doors.

"Hello there!" A voice shocked him from the shadows, a frank, childish voice.

Ezra Bradford stopped and set his jaw, turning slowly to his right. It seemed a boy was standing in the shadows near one of the book shelves. The boy spoke again. "Who are you?"

Ezra peered at him. "Why, I'm . . . Who are you?"

"I'm right here," said the boy, taking two steps forward. "I'm John. Who are you?"

"Pastor Ezra Bradford."

The boy stopped and stood. "Did you come to pray?"

"Well, no, I came to meet the board."

There was a brief silence. "You came to meet the Lord?"

"Well, no. The board."

"Only boards I know is over in the storage room. There's a pile of 'em over there. You need 'em?"

"No, no. The selection board . . . the committee for the new minister." Ezra felt embarrassed to be defending himself before a child. "Why are you here, son?"

"Always here on Fridays. Clean the place. Supposed to get it extra clean for the new minister who's comin' tomorrow."

"Tomorrow?"

"Yeah. In the afternoon."

"Did you ring the bell?"

He saw the boy's teeth appear as he smiled. "They let me ring the bell to let Mother Julia up the road know that I got finished with my cleaning."

"Mother Julia. Your mother?"

"No. Mommy died a while back. Mother Julia lives just over thataway." His thumb turned north. "She kind of keeps an eye on the place for the church elders. She used to go to this church a long time ago. She still comes over here on Fridays to pray. Says 3 'clock is the time Jesus died, so she walks on over here after I get done with my work. Should be here pretty soon. She locks up after I leave."

"How do you get to work?"

"Bike. I got a good bike with the money I saved up."

Ezra Bradford sighed. "Well, I suppose I've mistaken the day. You see, my wife passed away. She used to keep me on schedule."

"Yeah? So you're the minister that's comin' to take over after Pastor Mack left? He was a nice old guy."

"Well, no. I'm not taking over, just meeting with the committee."

"I think Mr. Matherson and the rest of 'em work most Fridays, so they ain't going to be here today . . . but I can show you around if you want. Except in there." He pointed into the sanctuary. "Mother Julia says not to go in there except to clean and pray. But over in the other part, the part that sticks out on both sides of the church? There's a whole bunch of stuff you're supposed to see."

"Supposed to see?

"Yeah. Mr. Matherson told me to get it extra clean today, even the storage place, 'cause he said you might want to look around. And there's some cool stuff there. He said they were going to let the new pastor decide what to do with all that stuff."

"Stuff?"

"Old books, a big tall candle, and they've got Big Jesus buried over there."

Ezra looked back sharply at the boy's upturned face, looking for mockery. But the boy's large, inquisitive eyes didn't change.

They's a little Jesus, too, up on the wall in that room. Nobody ever took him down. Anyways, I got the keys."

Ezra heard the jingle of a few keys the boy held up and could see John smiling in the shadows. Ezra raised his brows, then nodded. "Well, let's take a look. I evidently have plenty of time."

The boy first turned to the inner, sanctuary doors and took two wood wedges that lay in the shadows and propped open the inner narthex doors, kicking the wooden wedges into place with his heel. Ezra noticed he was barefoot. Then the boy turned, walked through the narthex, and pushed hard on the front doors. They whined on their hinges.

Outside the doors, the wind had died a little. Ezra saw that the boy was clothed in a dirty white t-shirt and cut-off jeans that reached just below his knees. Ezra squinted up at the sky. The dark clouds to the southwest were building high into a pale blue sky, shutting out the sun.

The boy jumped down the stairs and hurried toward the bell tower on their left. Ezra followed.

"The rope for the bell's in there," said the boy. He pointed at the bell tower and the wooden door at its base. "They let me ring it when I'm done," he repeated. Then he skipped quickly along a path around the tower and Ezra followed him down a path of beaten-down grass to the arched door of the transept where the boy inserted a key and unlocked the door.

As Ezra made his way toward him, the boy called out, "After I ring the bell for Mother Julia, I come and sit on the front steps waitin' for her. Sometimes takes her awhile. She's gettin' old. But I ain't seen her yet, so I started to go into the church to see if she was already here, but it was you that was already here. Kind of scared me at first." He held the door open for Ezra.

The boy flicked on a light switch. There was an open door into an unused office space to their left. Ezra could see a clean desk, empty bookshelves, and several chairs standing before a back window. The place was hot. Evidently they didn't use the air conditioner during the week. The center room looked like a Sunday School classroom; there was a standing whiteboard and maybe fifteen folding chairs. The boy walked to the right, inserted a key, and opened a door. He knelt quickly in the doorway, stood up, and looked back at Ezra. "Mother Julia says to do it. Deacon Matherson said I don't have to, but I kind of like to anyway. Mother Julia says it's because he's God. I sometimes think I ought to go down on my face, but I ain't never seen nobody do that before, not even Mother Julia."

The boy used his foot to shove away a mop bucket and motioned the minister in. Ezra stepped through the doorway. There, beyond the brooms, buckets, carnauba wax cans, a small stack of one-by-fours, and a pile of rags, lying across two wooden sawhorses, a man lay in the half light. It had been an anxious afternoon and Ezra Bradford started at first sight of the figure, its face and half-closed eyes turned toward the light from the doorway. But it was quite lifeless. Carved of a pale wood, the figure lay nailed to a five-foot cross of dark wood.

The boy stood and watched the minister's face as he walked over and inspected the body. It was an exquisite carving, the hair matted beneath the thorns, the torso twisted in agony, old stains running along the distended tendons of the arms.

"Mother Julia says it ain't right to bury him in here." The boy's voice was quiet. "If you was to be the new pastor, would you bring him back up? Mother Julia says he got raised right up out of the grave. Deacon Matherson says so too and that's why they won't put up a dead Jesus on the wall, but statues ain't alive nohow. Mother Julia says it's such a special statue 'cause it makes us remember. She says he departs a blessing."

"Imparts," corrected the minister. He was about to dispute the point but the boy went on.

"She's a good person to pray with, Mother Julia. I never much liked praying before I met her. She just sort of talks straight to him for a while and we both mention our concerns. That's what she calls 'em, 'concerns.' She has a bunch of concerns. Then we say the regular prayers together. She's got her beads to keep track of where we're at in the prayers."

The minister frowned.

"Deacon Matherson don't like them beads neither. You know, you two are going to get along real good."

"I'm glad you pray, John," said Ezra.

The ten-year-old turned on his heel and pulled open a tall oak wardrobe. "Look at this!" Inside, to the boy's obvious delight, hung a dusty, brocaded chasuble. Though it hung stiffly and had frayed along the hems, Ezra could still make out an intricate pattern of alternating golden roses and silver pomegranates stitched to a wine-red background interlaced with what appeared to be broken threads of gold.

"That's a very old and expensive robe," remarked the minister.

"Yeah, but Deacon Matherson says they don't want to sell it 'cause ministers ain't got no business wearing fancy robes. You don't wear nothin' as cool-lookin' as this do you?"

"No."

"Too bad. Jesus is supposed to be a king, right?"

Ezra Bradford could see the argument coming. "Yes, but when he lived on earth, he dressed very simply, just like everybody else, John."

"But nowadays you don't suppose he sits around in heaven with a suit on, do you?"

"I suppose you'd like to see me with that robe on?"

"You bet!" He paused and looked around the room. "So what are you going to do with all this here stuff?" There was a large white candle decorated with a painted cross but the candle had clearly never been lit. There were boxes of candle sticks. In a shadowed corner, a bearded saint leaned stiffly against a wall, its feet together, a statue of a woman robed in blue stood with the same posture, and Ezra knew these were the statues taken from the front chancel wall.

"I don't even have the job yet, John. I'd have to cross that bridge when I get there."

John's bright eyes looked solemnly at the minister. "Reverent, why don't you just put Big Jesus back up in the church?"

Thunder rumbled not far away. Ezra Bradford walked back through the room's doorway and then out through the arched stone doorway. The wind had died and there was a great stillness in the air. He thought he could smell the rain coming. "John, I'd better get going before the rain breaks loose. Can I give you a ride?"

The boy followed him out and closed the door, but didn't lock it. "No thanks, I got to find out what's going on with Mother Julia. Sometimes it takes her a while."

"All right, John. I'll be back tomorrow. Maybe I'll see you more in the days ahead."

"Sure," said the boy. "Hope it's you gets the job."

The minister said good bye and walked toward the bell tower. Rounding the tower, he glanced back at John standing framed in the transept door, still watching him. The ivy along the church wall fluttered in a sudden rain-scented breeze and Ezra turned and walked toward his car.

He opened its door and sat down. He sat there for a minute trying to decide what to do next. He had little desire to return to his motel. It was too early for dinner. He felt tired, annoyed with himself for not writing down the day of the appointment. It was such a quiet place, refreshing in its way, even stirring in its depiction of apostles, prophets, and martyrs. The first large drops of rain began to fall on the dust on his windshield.

He opened the car door, stepped out, and hurried back to the church.

Pulling open the big oak doors, he slipped back into the soft light of the narthex and closed the tall doors behind him. Another crack of thunder. He heard the rain begin in earnest.

He stepped through the wedged-open sanctuary doors and made his way to one of the back pews on the far left side. The place was now dark. A pale light emanated from the windows, but he could barely make out the front pews. He sat back and sighed. He felt as if there had always, ever, been silence here, as if, steeping through the decades, the stone, wood, and glass had long mediated a calm alternative to the rush and clash of the modern world. Perhaps this was the place he was intended to be in his later years. Perhaps he could raise the money to replace the sanctuary's back windows. He had always been an effective fund raiser.

He heard the entry doors squeak open and heard the rush of rain outside. Someone entered. The back doors whined shut. He turned, expecting to see young John again. Instead, the pale wooden crucifix passed through the tall narthex doors and rose to a position three feet from the floor. Once again his body started, and he gripped the carved armrest next to him. Then, with exaggerated and stately step, John's bare feet strode down the center aisle, the cross grasped firmly to his chest.

Ezra Bradford smiled at his fear. John had not seen him.

With measured step the boy carried the crucifix toward the eastern wall, up the steps, around the pulpit and to the back wall. There John leaned the cross against the wall and slid a folding chair over, picked up the cross, climbed onto the chair, and pressed the crucifix into the stone.

Ezra was surprised that it stayed on the stone. There must be long nails or fasteners of some kind that slid into the holes in the wall. The faint light from the windows was just enough to reveal a subtle image of Christ, like a ghost hovering there on the shadowed wall.

John stepped down, moved past the choir chairs and pulpit, and down the three steps where he turned and awkwardly knelt, crossed himself, rose, and walked again with measured steps down the center aisle. When he reached the sanctuary doors, he turned again, briefly bowed, and left. Ezra heard him push open the doors. The doors evidently caught and remained open for he did not hear them close. He could hear the rain falling.

Ezra Bradford closed his eyes and leaned back. Maybe he should pray. But before he could make up his mind, the boy called, "Pastor, you still here? I seen your car out there."

"Yes, John. Over here."

The boy stepped back into the sanctuary. "Hope you don't mind about Big Jesus. . . . Mother Julia and I always do this on Fridays. Only she ain't here yet. I'm going to run up the road and check on her. She lives alone, you know. I don't mind the rain."

The doors must have remained open, for he could still hear the steady rain and there was a fresh scent of the rain. It seemed cooler now . . . serene . . . he was tired. He closed his eyes and relaxed.

\+ \+ \+

He wasn't sure when his eyes opened, but the rain had stopped and the sun had returned, streaming again through the south windows. The old, stained figure on the cross seemed to animate a warm, ivory radiance on the shadowed wall. He felt strangely refreshed and slightly confounded. He looked about and yawned. The white window paint near him still obscured the figures. A fly buzzed against a pane of glass. Yet, by some unaccountable alchemy, he felt better, invigorated. Perhaps it was the nap. Again the sanctuary was radiant with haloed lights pouring through the southern windows, streaming through the illuminated figures of men and women long dead. He felt that in a way he had indeed intruded upon a service in progress, that the place was filled with decades of worship, that amid these dilapidated walls of old stone and plaster the generations of parishioners who had sat through countless services singing, worshipping, or dozing, were still in attendance. The devotion of decades of song and service seemed somehow distilled as he gazed upon the figure of the one he had served so long.

His heart lifted and he stood.

Perhaps he should sing. He felt that he should sing. So he did. One voice. Solitary but glad:

"Oh ye heights of heaven adore Him,
Angel hosts His praises sing,
Powers, dominions bow before Him,
And extol our God and King!
Let no tongue on earth be silent.
Every voice in concert ring!
Evermore and evermore . . . ."

The sound of his voice trailed away. All returned to stillness and solitude. He eased back down into the pew.

"You sure got a loud voice," came the boy's voice from the narthex.

Ezra turned about abruptly. "John! How long have you been here?"

"Mother Julia's not feeling so well, and with the rain and all, she decided not to come. She said I should lock things up."

Ezra nodded and got to his feet.

"But I gots to take Big Jesus back down and bury him. Mr. Matherson wouldn't like him up there."

"I understand."

John padded up the aisle in his bare feet. Ezra noticed his hair was soaked. The boy quickly knelt and rose, hurried up the steps to the chancel and took down the cross, then marched it down the aisle as before, dipped it to enter the narthex, and carried it away.

Ezra Bradford sat back down. Silence rested there like a familiar friend. Two crickets began conversing with each other across the sanctuary. After a minute or two, he stood back up and made his way to the entrance, stepped through the narthex doors, walked past the tables where he had met John, pushed open the creaky doors, and stepped out. The sun was setting across the cornfield. Light-winged swallows were dipping and turning in the early evening air. The clouds were gone. There was that fresh scent of rain and grass. He took off his suit coat, folded it and placed it on the damp rocks of the stone steps. He sat down.

John soon returned, went inside to pull the wedges and close the sanctuary doors, closed and locked the entry doors, and said goodbye to the minister. Ezra asked him if he needed a ride, but the boy said he had his bike.

Ezra watched him peddle beneath the tall, white-trunked sycamore tree, down the gravel driveway, then turn left down a little shortcut path that dipped into the roadside ditch. His bike splashed through a little running water. He stood on his peddles and pumped the bike up onto the gravel road and peddled away.

Ezra spent another hour walking about the grounds, reading the inscriptions on the gravestones, wandering about. He decided to stay and watch the sun set. He took his folded suitcoat and shook out the wrinkles as best he could, put it in his car and returned to the steps.

After a while, the sun set. It was a gentle evening, cooler now. The swallows had gone to their nests. In time stars began to appear. He sat there on the stone steps trying to sort his thoughts and emotions. After a while he pushed himself to his feet. Warm lights blinked through the oak trees to the north. He thought that must be Mother Julia's house near the church. Perhaps he could convince her to come to services. He'd like to meet her.

Perhaps he could persuade the members of the congregation to remove Aquinas and hire an artist to replace him with . . . . Well, Luther wouldn't do for a Baptist congregation, nor Knox. Maybe Zwingli? Maybe Wesley? But not for Baptists. . . . maybe John the Baptist? He pulled at his chin. Who could balance Augustine? And Ambrose? Perhaps they could remove the crown from Mary in the circular window and replace the rest of her and her son's figures? We don't have anything against the virgin birth, he said to himself, but the plywood has got to go.

Long into the night, while the high stars turned in their bright patterns, he waited and watched.

Drifting

Looking for Pablo Riz

He found his eyes following a football game reflected upside down and backwards in a four-inch square on a glass table top. He had no idea who was playing. No desire to look up at the overhead television screen to find out. The little padded midgets were grouping together in their four-inch world, lining up, then exploding into motion, their tiny feet rushing silently across their white-striped green ceiling.

He looked at the paper cup of coffee. Untouched. He slid the cup of cold, black decaf over the square reflecting the football game. A prism of colors rippled across the surface of coffee and slowly settled into a black reflection of upside down little figures rushing back and forth, forth and back, running on coffee.

The Daily Grind coffee shop was the only one that stayed open till nine in the evening in his section of Kansas City. The place used to be a bank, and the old vault door on the back wall, with its complicated locking mechanisms, stood open. They had made the inside of the vault into a children's playroom so adults could sit at tables in the main room and enjoy their coffee confections in peace. The first time he walked into this coffee shop and saw the open bank vault, he had stopped and smiled. The fact that a bank's secured vault, shut and locked to protect the world of serious business from intruders, would now lie open to the games of children had appealed to him. He remembered mornings when he used to bring his daughter Jessica here when she was a toddler. He had been doing independent graphic design work for customers while his wife was finishing nursing school, so he would drive little Jessica here and let her create block houses in the playroom while he sipped caffeinated coffee and brainstormed ideas for his clients. That was years ago. His daughter had now become a rather sarcastic middle schooler whose main interests involved her school friends.

Three others were sitting out the evening in the coffee shop: the barista behind the counter, staring into her phone, her manicured finger flicking at the screen and two women talking at a nearby table.

He had slept little the night before. He stared out into the darkness of early winter traffic, then looked at his wristwatch: 8:33 p.m. He needed to brainstorm ideas before the place closed in half an hour.

His eyes moved to his open sketch pad lying on the table.

His client wanted a cover design for a new brand of spring water in biodegradable cartons that would replace plastic. The next big thing in bottled water. Eco-friendly.

He stared at the blank sheet and began sketching in the face and torso of the woman at the adjacent table who was gabbling away world without end to the young woman opposite her who kept nodding her head to her companion's endless complaints.

Three years ago he had left the best advertising firm in Kansas City to start his own graphic design studio. He had plenty of clients. He worked with two medical centers, local work for a national telephone service, designing last year's banners for the Kansas City Chiefs football organization. He paid a secretary to take care of the billing and paperwork and an enthusiastic college grad to produce the ordinary lettering, the simpler designs, the newsletters and small ads, while he, Foster Ulysses Turner, was the creative guy who had won seven ADDY awards in Kansas City and two regional golds.

But how do you keep churning out creativity 47 weeks a year?

He would come up with three or four options for every customer. You could damn well depend on mid-level managers to choose the least creative design, or some hotshot, who fancied himself artistic, would jump in at the last minute to move the lettering a quarter inch to the left or change the tint of the background. Or some arts manager on her way up the company ladder would insist that the lettering wasn't "friendly enough." Friendly lettering. He remembered glancing at her and saying, "The reason it's not friendly enough is that the lettering has not yet experienced the loyalty and self sacrifice required of lasting relationships." She had laughed; he had not. One didn't keep customers with such behavior.

He no longer cared. "Change it," he would say. "We're not talking Michelangelo, Matisse, or Sonbouleé here." Years before he'd follow this with, "You do know Sonbouleé, don't you?" Some clients nodded yes, some no. He would shrug and move on. He'd made up the name. Sometimes it was Sonbouleé, sometimes Gonzalo de Cartagena, sometimes Sanya Vizhenski—whatever came to mind. They were selling bottled water for God's sake. Or packaged pizza. This wasn't high art, but oh yes, the capital letter needed to be "just a hair larger, wouldn't you say?" and the color of the water must be "just a smidgen lighter, don't you think? Need to keep it happy looking, don't ya think?"

He stared at the cream-colored marble wall three feet from his table, polished stone imbedded with veins of brown that trickled off this way and that, looking like congealed mud.

He glanced at his watch: 8:40.

He returned to his sketch, expanding the woman's waistline, adding a double chin.

"Snap out of it, Foster," his wife would say. "Go somewhere. Do something!"

Once, after work, on a summer afternoon, he had left his office and walked up a residential street ringing doorbells. Each time someone came to the door, Foster asked for Pablo Riz. No one had heard of anyone named Pablo Riz. (He had checked the Kansas City metropolitan area phone book to make sure the name Riz did not exist.) If no one answered the doorbell, he'd try the door. After thirty or forty tries, he found one unlocked and stepped in. No one around. He turned on the television, sat down on the couch, and watched mindless comedies for two hours until someone drove into the two-car garage. He heard the car door shut and then a man opened the kitchen door, walked in, and gasped. Foster pushed himself to his feet and held out his hand. "I was looking for Pablo Riz," he said.

"Who?"

"Pablo, Pablo Riz." He rolled the *r*.

The man was a bit overweight, dressed in khaki slacks and a pale blue shirt. "No, no. I'm not. . . How did you get in?"

Foster had smiled and apologized. "Thought you left the door open for an old friend. But I must have the wrong address," he said. He had shrugged and walked out the front door. But even such chaotic behavior didn't calm the dull anxiety that nagged him.

Every weekday morning at nine o'clock he walked into his office, said hi to his two employees, checked over the endless, self-reproducing paper work for an hour or so, then, at what he used to call the golden hour, sat down at his computer to crank out the creativity.

In The Daily Grind, the time was now 8:45. He stared at his watch, its visible rotating mechanisms clicking back and forth.

He used an eraser to put the now obese woman on a diet, but added a triple chin.

His wife Carol would say, "Come on, Foster. Find a different job. Travel. Find a woman. You never look at *me* anymore!" She had moved to her mother's home just three months before and had taken their thirteen-year-old Jessica with her.

\+ \+ \+

He found himself sitting alone on his overstuffed leather chair with the lights out in his Kansas City apartment. He stared up at the textured ceiling. Carol had just called, informing him that he had missed his appointment to take Jessica to the latest Disney production. As Carol was pleading with him, he had reached into his pocket and pulled out a bright new quarter. He and Jessica had been putting together a complete collection of the state quarters. Their rule was that you couldn't go to the bank, but had to find them in the course of everyday life. The little game had Jessica commandeering every handful of change he or Carol obtained and searching for the quarters. He had recently found Idaho with its vigilant falcon and had intended to let Jessica find it before the movie, but time had moved on without him.

"Foster, she depends on you. She was so looking forward to this."

"I'm sorry. I truly am."

"What happened? What's going on in that head of yours?"

He refused to answer. She ended up barking, "Go somewhere, Foster! Anywhere. Just get out of here till you get yourself together. I can't stand to be around you anymore! And neither can Jessica! She's in her bedroom bawling."

The phone clicked off.

Twilight had already darkened the sixth-floor apartment, so he reached over and clicked his desk lamp on. The place was quiet but for the steady breathing of the furnace. He opened a book to his self-designed bookmark: a black crow sitting in the winter crown of a distant cottonwood tree, rendered on thick white cardstock. He liked that bird. Crows were chaotic: rising on the wind, flinging out their harsh cries. Free to fly, free to shout, free to swerve and dive and soar and laugh. He placed the bookmark on the coffee table, took a sip of bourbon and began reading.

After five minutes, Foster closed the book and laid it down. He put his head back again and stared at the ceiling. The ceiling textures gradually took on the appearance of winter fields, white, flat fields grooved in half-circle patterns that looked like plow marks that repeated themselves to the shadowed walls.

\+ \+ \+

He found himself walking a dirt and gravel road 60 miles west of Kansas City. The rural roads of northeastern Kansas don't turn and twist, following ridgelines like the roads in Virginia where Foster grew up. Here the national grid insisted on running farm roads north to south, east to west, imposing its gridiron on the landscape, which meant that Foster with his backpack and wide-brimmed camping hat would stride quickly down a long slope and then climb the facing hill. He had always worked out every noon hour in the local gym and jogged most every evening, so the long walk hadn't been that difficult initially, but the soles of his feet were getting sore. He hadn't counted on that.

He had spent the first night in his two-person tent in the company of his backpack. He had walked into a pasture and found a secluded spot behind a grove of oak and hackberry trees. The weather was mild and four or five calves had joined him for the night. He could hear them cropping the grass and shuffling curiously about his tent till he fell asleep. Another night he awoke to a cold wind shaking his tent and coyotes not far away breaking into a chorus of yips and barks and wailing. Their wild calls caught at his heart and he started to shout and bark and howl. The coyotes went silent.

This morning he was out of the tent and pacing along before sunrise chewing on another piece of beef jerky. A front had moved through in the night, warming things a bit, but early December in Kansas was still cold and he had his wool vest and winter jacket zipped to his chin, his now rumpled camping hat pulled down to his eyebrows. Except for his sore feet, it felt good to stride down a gentle rise with the sun just rising behind him. His backpack carried a water canister, a bottle of water purification tablets, a sleeping bag, a small container of cooking gear, plastic-wrapped sheathes of beef jerky, the tent and sleeping pad, and a roll of toilet paper. He had left his car on a gravel road that fishermen used in summer to access the Missouri River and had walked away along a two-lane blacktop for miles, but had been annoyed by passing trucks and cars and had left the highway near Valley Falls and taken to the gravel farm roads.

The road he was walking followed a shallow stream. Thick leafless brush climbed banks that obscured the clear current. Walnut trees, white-trunked sycamores, oaks, and tall cottonwood trees stood overhead, the bare limbs intersecting, twisting, tangled like the complicated scribble-sketch rendered by an angry artist. Only the oaks held an occasional patch of dry, brown leaves rattling and rustling in the cool breeze. A stand of brown burdock and dried nettles beside the road trembled. He had learned the names of all these trees and plants while taking extended hikes with his little brother in Virginia. A biology teacher at the local high school had forced his class to collect leaves from a nearby cemetery and name the plants. It had become his favorite high school class. On frequent hikes and campouts, he had started teaching his little brother the names: lambsquarter, jewelweed, sumac, poison pokeberry.

Now, he had thought a winter hike would clear his mind and settle his heart.

He saw a small, white, two-story house off to his right through a veil of young grey trees. He was hungry. He'd had more than enough of beef jerky and wanted to see if he could buy some canned goods from a local farmer. He walked up the gravel drive to the front porch, stepped up three stone steps, removed a glove, and knocked.

A boy opened the door. Maybe twelve or thirteen, about the same age as his Jessica. He was a thin boy in jeans and a black t-shirt with a Kansas City Chiefs red logo. Wide eyes peered up at him. He had a freckled nose and his hair was an unruly mess. "My mom's not here," he said.

"I'm looking for Pablo Riz," Foster said.

The boy looked down, then looked up again. "I don't think I've ever heard that name around here."

"Really? I thought he lived around here."

The boy frowned and shook his head. "Not that I know of."

"Well," said Foster, "I'm out hiking and am running out of my food supplies, so I was wondering if I could buy some cans of food from you."

The boy thought about it for a second. "I don't think my mom would want me to let you in. At least I'd have to call and ask her."

"I'd be glad to pay for the food," Foster offered, but the boy said, "If you're really hungry, I can bring out some canned beans or something. My mom might be mad if I didn't offer you anything."

"No, that's all right. I'll try down the road somewhere."

"Maybe stewed tomatoes, or maybe Spam or something? We have some of that."

Foster looked at the inquiring eyes and thought the boy must be lonely. "Aren't you supposed to be in school?"

"My mom teaches me at night and gives me stuff to work on in the daytime."

"All right. Thanks anyway."

He left the boy standing at the open door."

He returned to the road that still followed the thin current of the clear-running stream beneath its attendant cottonwoods and oaks. It was good to walk. He tried to keep his mind away from using the landscape to plot graphic designs for waiting clients.

In time he spotted a greyish house to his right. A two-track gravel driveway with dried weeds and crumpled grasses running between the tracks curved past the house of peeling clapboards to a wide, red, one-story barn with a slightly sloped roof. Its open portals held cultivators, a farm trailer, a small combine, a fishing boat. He walked up the drive. A harvested soybean field lay to his left, the low-cut stalks standing pale grey in the morning light. He passed a couple of goats that watched him from behind a six-foot wire mesh fence. He walked around a dented old pickup truck parked near the front door and stepped onto weathered planking of a covered porch and pushed the doorbell with a gloved hand. No sound. A dog began barking inside. He took off the glove and knocked.

It sounded like a small dog yapping. Someone inside barked at the dog and shuffled to the front door. An old man opened the door holding in his arm the little brown Chihuahua mix that started barking again. He was a grim old man in a soiled grey sweatshirt and baggy jeans. The dog wouldn't shut up, so the man placed his fingers around its muzzle to keep it quiet.

Foster said, "I'm looking for Pablo Riz."

"What?" The man turned his ear toward Foster. He had a small hooked nose with deep wrinkles around eyes and mouth.

"I'm looking for Pablo Riz."

"Never heard of him. He don't live nowheres near here." The dog jerked its muzzle from his hand and began yapping again.

"Well, I'm sorry to bother you. He's a friend of mine and I thought he lived somewhere around here. I'm out hiking and thought I'd surprise him."

The man had a stocking cap pulled down to his big ears and long jowls with a stubble of beard of about the same unkempt appearance as Foster's own beard. Foster hadn't shaved since he left the city.

"You ain't tanned enough to be a leather tramp. Your car broke down somewheres?"

"No. Just hiking. But I could use some canned goods. I'm tired of chewing on beef jerky for four days. I'd be glad to pay you for some canned pork and beans, maybe some canned tomatoes, a can of Spam?"

The man stood and stared. The dog stopped barking and sniffed and licked his master's stubbly cheek. "Well, I do got some of that. Pay me, you say?"

"Sure." Foster pulled his billfold from a hip pocket and handed the man two twenties. "That should cover a few cans."

The man's blue-veined hand reached out and took the money. "Okay. That'll work. Come on in."

He put the dog down on the floor and it began backing away and yapping again as the man led Foster through a dusty living room. A coffee table held a disassembled gear box of some sort, a few rags. The living room had the smell of oil and of the man's body odor, but the kitchen smelled of fresh coffee as they walked in. The man opened a pantry door and told Foster to take a look. Foster picked out a cylindric cardboard container of oatmeal and shook it. Mostly full. He took some canned vegetables, Spam, two cans of evaporated milk, pork and beans. He stuffed them all in his backpack as the man watched.

"That good?" he said to the man.

"You can take a few more. You gave me forty bucks."

"No, that's plenty. Don't want to get too weighted down." Foster shouldered his backpack and turned to go.

"Want some coffee? Pretty cold out there this time of mornin'," said the old man.

Foster smiled and let the backpack slip to the floor. "I could sure use hot coffee."

The man took the pot from an electric coffee maker and poured coffee into an old enameled tin cup. He handed it to Foster, who asked if the man had any cream. The man opened the refrigerator and handed him a glass jar half full of milk.

"It's goat milk. Hope that don't bother you none."

Foster poured it in and took a sip. "Different," he said. "So, are you retired?"

"You got that right. I get up every damn morning and face the wreakage of the future," he said without smiling.

Foster nodded, taking another sip of the strong, goat-flavored coffee.

The man sat down on a stool next to his formica countertop and motioned Foster to sit.

Foster took the next stool and sat, unzipping his heavy jacket and taking off his hat and laying it on the counter.

"You know?" said the man, "I don't count for much at all around here. Don't amount to a hill of beans. Wife's long gone, kids gone, nothing but little Hiram here to keep me company."

The little dog looked up at the sound of its name.

"But I'm about all I think about most of the time. How weird is that?"

"Sounds normal to me," said Foster.

"It don't sound right to me," said the man as he stood up and poured himself a cup. He took the jar of goat milk and added it to his coffee. "You need sugar?" he asked. "I should've asked, but I'm not much used to visitors."

"Sure."

The man pushed a ceramic container decorated with faded blue flowers across the formica countertop and handed Foster a spoon. The cabinets were the old white-enameled metal cabinets of a bygone era.

"Where you headed?" the man asked.

"West."

The man took back the sugar and stirred in a spoonful.

"No destination?"

"Not yet."

"Where you comin' from?"

They fell into conversation. Foster sipping his cup of coffee, the old man in his sweatshirt sitting on the stool with the dog at his feet. Foster told him he was out to take a look at life. Clear his mind.

The man said, "Well, I never had much time for that most days, but now I got too much time."

"You have a television?" Foster asked.

"Even I know that's mostly a waste. Had a friend once that went to college over there at KU. Said he read a truckload of books when he was in college. Graduated, come home to his pretty little wife. Lived in a trailer house out south of Topeka, kept a few goats which is the reason I got to know him. Said one day he was settin' on his couch watchin' something and stopped and asked hisself what the hell he was doin'. Gone to college all them years and read great books and now was wastin' his life on that television shit. So he gets hisself up, unplugs the tv, carries it outside, grabs ahold of his shotgun and blasts it to smithereens. Never had a television since. One of the most interesting guys I ever knowed. Plays in a Irish band, raised three sons, talked to me one day in a bar about some philosopher name of Spitnoza or something, somebody I never heard about before or since. Raised goats too, like I said."

"So you don't have a television?"

"Oh, no. I got one. How can you avoid 'em? But about all I watch is the evening news, which makes me mad, and weather which makes me worry, and sports to get my heart thumpin' again. I watch a helluva lot of sports."

+ + +

With the oatmeal and ten or eleven cans in his backpack, Foster found himself back on the road that still followed the stream. The sun was up casting his long walking shadow ahead of him. He heard someone running up the gravel road behind him and turned. It was the boy again, but now he had on a heavy tan jacket and a faded Kansas City Royals baseball cap. He ran up and stopped, breathing hard. "Did you stop in to see old man Robinson?"

"I don't know. Never got his name."

"That's Robinson all right. Nice old guy. Not so happy, though." He was still panting. "I thought you must have gone to him for some food or something."

"You like the old man?"

"He's not a very happy man."

"Are you?"

"I'm a boy."

"I can see that. Aren't boys allowed to be happy?"

"Yeah, sure." He took a deep breath and looked away through the trees. "I'd say I'm happy most days."

They began walking.

"There's not much company out here with my mom away for work, but I keep myself busy most days." The boy slid his hands deep into his jean pockets. His nose was red and his freckled cheeks flushed. "Yes!"

"Yes what?"

"I'd have to say I think I'm mostly happier than lots of people."

"You are? Why?"

"I like lots of things."

"Like what?" They were passing under three tall, bare cottonwoods.

"I make up games," the boy said.

"Like what?"

"I ask questions."

"Questions?"

"Like where are you going?"

"I don't know."

"Are you walking away from something or walking toward something?"

"Just walking. . . So what lies up this road?"

They walked on a few steps. "If you go all the way out past Clay Center to Cawker City, there's the world's largest ball of twine."

"Why would I want to see that?"

"If you asked the right questions, it might be fun."

"Okay. What are the right questions?" They began walking up a hill. The stream had left the road and wandered away to their left, the line of leafless trees following the stream away from the road. A narrow cornfield cut to dry stalks a foot high lay between stream and road. Tall silver-seeded grasses stood along the ditches on either side. The weedy ditch to their right had a stand of leafless sumac holding clutches of clotted red-brown seeds nodding atop each thin limb.

"What's the right question?" Foster asked again.

"Maybe, why would anybody make a 20-ton ball of twine?"

"Okay, why?"

"No, I asked the question. You have to answer it."

"Okay. Because someone's a total idiot."

"I think there's a better answer."

Foster shifted his backpack with the new cans of food in it as he climbed the hill. Their long shadows walked before them. "That was my answer. You have a better one?"

"I'm thinking it must have been an accident. Some old farmer starts collecting pieces of bailing twine, and he wraps it up in a ball and hangs it on a nail in his barn to use up later, but he never sorts it out into lengths he can use again. Then it gets too big for the nail. Then, after a while the neighbors start commenting on this 20-year-old ball of twine on his barn floor, but the guy who never throws anything away can't get himself to get rid of it. After a while it becomes some kind of game."

"Game."

"Yeah, you know. The neighbors keep commenting on it and he thinks it's funny and keeps on collecting to see how big it gets. Maybe they start bringing him wads of string to make it bigger. Isn't that why you've worked jobs all your life, so you could have fun hiking?"

"I have worked hard all my life so I could keep working hard all my life."

"Then what's the point?"

"What's the point? You know the point. Money."

"And how has that worked out for you?" The boy raised his freckled face and looked at Foster as they climbed the hill. "You know," the boy said, "Plato said that play was the most important thing in life."

"Plato?" Foster looked down at the baseball cap. "You read philosophy?"

"I read lots of stuff. My mom home schools me at night when she gets off work. I have lots of time to read, and I like it."

"So what did Plato have to say about play?"

The hill was getting steeper, so Foster slowed.

"Plato said, 'To be sure'—that's the way he said it—'To be sure, man's life is a business that doesn't deserve to be taken seriously.' Isn't that amazing? I mean, Plato, as I'm sure you know, is considered a very serious guy."

"I haven't read him since college."

"So then he goes on to say that what's really serious is play. That we should really pay attention to important things like play."

"Okay."

"Yeah, he said we should live out our time by playing games, sacrificing, singing, dancing, stuff like that."

"Sacrificing?"

"You know, I asked my mom about that. She read the pages I was reading and said that singing and dancing and sacrificing were, 'apparently'—she always says, 'apparently' when she's not for sure on something, so 'apparently,' dancing and sacrificing were part of their worship of the gods. Anyway, so he said we should not waste our life on trifles. That's the word he used, 'trifles,' which I had to look up because nobody uses that word much anymore. It means stupid little things that aren't worth much."

"Like building a huge ball of twine."

"No, but that's okay, you see? Because he made it into a game that people enjoyed. People pay money to watch games. You watch football, don't you?"

"Sometimes."

"Well, I really look forward to watching football—every week this time of year. It's more important to me than my school work."

"So what else do you read?"

"Lately I've been reading thoughts."

"Thoughts."

"Yes, it's a book called *Thoughts*."

"Just a book of random thoughts?"

"Yeah, but they make you think. He's another old guy. Lived back in France a long time ago. I guess he was going to put all the thoughts together in an organized book, but he died before he could get it all done. So they're all just kind of wound up together."

"Like a ball of twine."

The boy laughed out loud. "Yes! Like that."

"So he was just collecting thoughts like that old farmer collected random bits of string?"

"I guess, but his thoughts really make you think. It's a book that's part of my mom's Harvard collection of great books."

"Does your mom make you read this?"

"No, but she's got a pretty good library. She and my dad had quite a collection. She lets me pick out any book I want. Then we talk about it that night. She wants to know what I learned. She told me once she was getting a better education from me than she did in college, but I think she was just saying that."

"What happened to your dad?"

He shuffled along for a few steps and said, "Car accident when I was six. . . . I don't like to think about it."

"Okay."

They were approaching the top of the hill. Foster stopped walking and looked back. The gentle valley beneath was marked by the tree-lined stream that wound away to the south and blonde dry-grass hills that rose to the horizon, patched with stands of grey trees and dark-green junipers. "So you read some old guy's thoughts."

"How long do you think those cottonwoods down there can live?"

"This is one of that old guy's questions?"

"No, it's mine, but it seems like every question leads to some thought that old guy wrote down."

"Okay."

"So, how old?"

"I have no idea."

"You've got to try to answer or the game doesn't work."

"Cottonwoods? I don't know, maybe a hundred years or so, maybe more?"

"So the cottonwoods live longer than us?"

"I expect so."

"So does that make them greater than us?

"Greater. What do you mean, greater?"

"Just answer the question."

"Just being old doesn't make you great."

"Right! So they say the universe we can see is maybe thirteen to fifteen billion years old, maybe more. Doesn't that make the universe greater than a tree?"

"It makes it older, but age, you already said, doesn't make something greater."

"Right!" The boy looked up with a big smile. "You didn't try to dodge the question. I think you might be good at this. Now that we answered the question about age, we can start defining greatness. It's your turn."

"My turn for what?"

"To ask a question."

"Any question?"

"Well, it's more interesting if we keep going along the same line of thought."

"Okay, then obviously, the next question is what makes something great." Foster began walking down the rise.

"Yes!" The boy gave a little skip and looked out to where the road's summit gently fell away a hundred yards then rose again on a higher hill. "I can stuff that whole universe of galaxies and black holes and planets and moons and stuff into my head, so I'm thinking that I'm greater than a universe that can't think at all."

"That's pretty smart, kid."

"Well, I didn't come up with that. The French guy did. He said that space swallows us up like tiny specks, but since it can't think, we are greater. You know what else he said?"

"You're about to tell me."

"He said that our greatness comes from knowing we're wretched. A tree doesn't know it's wretched; it's conscious of nothing much beyond maybe a feeling for roots and rain and stuff if it even feels that. But humans know they are wretched and that's what makes them great."

Foster stopped and considered the distances ahead. He returned his attention to the boy and asked, "Doesn't being wretched mean you're anything but great?"

"I didn't say great in everything, just greater than the universe."

"Greater than the entire universe?"

"Greater than the non-thinking parts."

"And what are the thinking parts?"

"You know that! Us."

"How about aliens?"

"Like in the movies?"

"Sure, but there might really be aliens out there in the stars."

"Maybe. But the movies make them out to be other versions of us, don't you think? Thinking things that act a lot like us. And we don't even know if they really exist, so I like to spend my time on us, who are bigger than trifles."

"That's reasonable. So how does this French guy, whose name we should come up with sometime, get away with telling us we're greater than the universe but still wretched?"

"Because we die and know it."

"So doesn't that make us less than a universe that never dies? "We already said that age doesn't make something great."

"You got me there. So what good does being great do us if we die?"

The boy pulled a wadded handkerchief from his coat pocket and blew his nose. "This cold makes my nose drip," he said. "Anyway, that's the right answer. That's the question. He says we are thinking reeds, weak little plants with big brains. We don't have a whole lot of reeds around here, except in the ponds, so I like to think of us as weeds, thinking weeds with big old thinking cabbages on top.

Foster smiled.

"The universe can kill us," the boy announced, "but we would still be greater than our killer."

"But still wretched?"

"Yes, but greater than the stars."

"Don't you need to get home, kid?"

"Don't you like the game?" The boy looked up at him as they made their way down the road, the dry-grass hills rising behind and beside—a stand of dark green junipers approached on the right and a grey, brushy ravine on the left.

"Okay, kid. So now we know that stars can't think and that we are wretches."

"Yes. But dignified wretches," the boy said. "So our dignity comes from the fact that we can think, but lots of times we don't think much. What do you think about most of the time?"

Foster was wondering where he could find a place to eat. "Are there any towns up this road? Any places to eat?"

"No. Didn't you get some food from old man Robinson?"

"Yes, but nothing ready to eat."

"I guess you could come back to my place and cook it."

"That's not happening. Your mom would object."

The boy thought about it and agreed. "So what do you think a lot about?" the boy asked again.

"Work," he said. "Maybe a lot about myself. That's what old man Robinson said this morning, and I think that's what most of us think about, our own concerns."

"So why do you think that is? said the boy.

"Because we're damned selfish," I suppose.

"Yes!" The boy skipped three times down to where the road began to rise again, turned, and waited for Foster. "Which makes us pretty wretched, wouldn't you say? I mean here are these cosmic cabbages walking around who can think about everything: math, science, history, family, the gods, and on and on, and we sit around thinking about ourselves."

"Gods? You said you didn't mess with aliens, because we can't examine them."

"But the gods are everywhere in old books. People were always messing with the gods or being messed with by the gods."

They walked up the next rise. It was a long, steep rise and Foster said nothing till they came to the top of the hill where they could see the road drop away into a larger valley of scattered cornfields and pastures. They stood there panting for a minute, then walked over the crest and began descending the slope.

"I guess the old guys did talk a lot about the gods," said Foster, "but aren't gods just imaginative creations, like aliens?"

"Plato and all those prophets in the Bible thought they were as real as rain, maybe a lot more real. Those guys were real interested in reality. That's Plato's definition of truth, you know."

"His definition?"

"Yeah, truth is that which is. That's what he said. So they wouldn't spend much time talking about that which isn't."

"But maybe," Foster said, "the gods were just a part of their cultural expectations, imaginative constructions."

The boy's baseball cap stopped and turned up. "Imaginative constructions. Those are cool words."

"Okay, so what do you think of 'imaginative constructions'?"

They stood on the road and heard a vehicle coming over the hill and soon a grey pickup truck crested the hill and headed down the rise. They stepped to the ditch and waited for the pickup to pass them. The driver raised two fingers from the steering wheel as he passed and left them in a cloud of white dust. They stood in the dust for a few moments then continued strolling down the hill.

"Well," the boy said, "like I said, the great thinkers from back then, including that *Thoughts* guy, think that dealing with the gods is the most important thing a wretched being can do. We are thinking weeds that keep nodding at the sun."

"Your French guy come up with that line?"

"Not exactly. I guess I came up with it. Anyway, it's got to be more than imagination or it's not worth wasting our game on."

"So you like thinking about the gods?"

"Of course! Have you read Homer's poems about the fall of Troy and stuff?"

"I've seen the movie."

"Not the same. Not the same. In the poems, the gods are all over the place and they expect sacrifices and worship from the humans."

"What if I don't believe in any of that."

"What's greater?"

"Greater than what?"

The boy found a hedge apple lying in the shallow ditch beneath a roadside tree of bare, twisted limbs, and began kicking the hard green ball, about the size and shape of a softball, down the road. "Wouldn't the universe be even greater if there were gods and if we owed them our lives?"

"Maybe. Depending if they really existed and we weren't worshipping illusions."

"Say there were different levels of gods," the boy said, "because we can see that the old Greek gods were kind of wretched. You know, hating each other and fighting each other and lying to each other, turning soldiers into pigs, that kind of stuff, so they were, 'apparently,'" he made air quotes with his fingers, "according to my mom, morally bad. So what if there were good powers and higher real forms? Like Plato said."

"That would be better and greater, but if it's an illusion, it's all a lie."

"Haven't you ever read the four god spells?"

"The what?"

They walked up to the dusty, yellow-green hedge apple and the boy gave it a hard kick that sent it bouncing into the far ditch. The boy turned to look at Foster. "You went to college and never read them?"

"I don't know what you're talking about."

"Well, that's the word the old English called them."

"You're an arrogant little shit sometimes, aren't you?"

"Why, because I read?"

"Maybe. What about these spells?"

"When you read them the god they talk about seems smart and sad."

"Does the god die?"

"Yes."

"So he's a wretched thinking weed like the rest of us."

"But it doesn't seem like it when you read about him—and besides, he doesn't stay dead."

"Well, I guess gods can do all sorts of supernatural things, which is why I never really believed in them."

"But what if they exist?"

"How would you ever find out?"

"Do you know about the incorruptibles?"

"You're sure as hell going to tell me."

The boy looked up and smiled, ran to the other side of the road, picked up the hard hedge apple from the thatch of dead grasses where it lay with its puckered, dusty, yellow-green skin, and rolled it like a bowling ball down the center of the road where it bounced and swerved on gravel to where the road began again to rise.

"I was reading this travel book," the boy said, "by a British travel writer named Thubron. He was traveling in Russia after Russia became Russia again and not the Soviet Union anymore. So, he came across this old church that had the body of some old saint in it. This guy, Thubron, said that when the Soviets controlled the place they didn't like it because it was a place pilgrims came to all the time to pray. So they broke open the casket that had a body that had never rotted in it. The saint had died more than thirty years before. So, the communists took the body outside someplace and buried it in the dirt. Well, some of the local people saw where it was buried. Sixty years later, after the Soviets had become Russians again, the people went and dug up the saint's body and it was still incorrupt!" The boy turned and faced Foster. "Sixty years of summer and winter and still not rotted. So they took it back and put it in the church again. What do you think of that?"

"Well, kid, there's a fool born every minute."

"You don't believe me?"

"I believe you read the story."

"Well, you could prove it right or prove it wrong."

"And how would you do that?"

"Find the church. Check it out. That guy who wrote the book wasn't even a believer, but he was honest enough to tell the story. Besides, there's a new incorrupt body over in Missouri now. My mom took me to see her. A black lady who was a nun, buried four years in the mud and dirt in a wood casket that broke and let the mud in, and she's still there like the day she was buried."

Foster said nothing.

"I was reading this other book, because I got interested in this stuff, and found out there are over 200 of these incorruptibles all over and that they are all Catholic or Orthodox saints—no Hindus or Buddhists or atheists."

"How about the famous body of Lenin in Moscow?"

"That's different. They won't allow a scientific investigation of it, but the incorruptibles have been checked out many times by scientists. The body of a French Catholic girl I read about is amazing. I've seen a color picture of her. She was a peasant girl from France. A bunch of nuns washed her body after years in a casket cause it got dusty. But it still hadn't rotted. And is still there."

"So you and your mom are Catholics?"

"Sure. There's no good reason not to be."

"You really are an arrogant little kid sometimes."

The boy smiled, turned, and made his way to the dusty hedge apple and gave it a kick up the rising road. "Maybe you're right," he said. "I guess I read too much."

Foster joined him as he kicked the hedge apple again.

"But if you don't read much, how are you supposed to ask the right questions?"

"A hell of a lot of smart people read a lot and don't ask the questions you come up with."

The boy turned and looked at Foster.

Foster walked on. The boy trotted to catch up.

"So you don't want to play the game anymore?" he asked as he came up alongside.

"Don't you play soccer or baseball, like an ordinary kid?"

"Sure, when I can find somebody to play with or my cousins come over."

"So you read books."

"My mom doesn't buy me video games, so I have to make up games. Isn't that okay?"

"Of course it is."

"So do you want another question?"

"Not really. I already understand I'm a wretched weed with a cabbage head."

"But that's only the beginning idea of the French guy. He goes on to all kinds of cool stuff."

"I'm sure he does."

"I was thinking." The boy slid his hands back into his pockets and paced down the hill. "What if I just met you and, like in the old books, you were actually some kind of hero and looking for that Pablo guy was code for trying to find some god that got lost around here or something. Wouldn't that be totally cool?"

"Believe me, I'm no kind of hero."

"Or what if you were sent out to find this Pablo guy and he turned out to be me, and you were on your way to kill me!"

"You're getting carried away, kid."

"Not really."

"I thought you didn't want to waste time on trifles like made up stories."

"But the French guy says stuff like this is really true."

"That I could be a hero or a devil."

"Yes."

"You're going crazy, kid."

"That French guy isn't crazy. He created the first computer-like calculator hundreds of years ago and was a great mathematician. So what if a tree could think and as we passed by, it knew *you* were a great hero and tried to kill you!"

"Now you have a thinking tree?"

"That would make the story much more interesting, wouldn't it? And if the tree was some horrible old demon and the stranger was really a god and didn't know it, wouldn't that make the story more important?"

"It would lack the necessary ingredient of reality."

"Yes!" The boy leaped in the air and did a half turn landing on his feet facing Foster. "You're playing the game the right way! But, according to the French guy, the whole point of being a meaningless thinking weed is that we were born to be gods! So, in a way, my story is not a trifle."

He walked on a few yards, turned and said, "So, if you're hungry, what's that say about you?"

Foster had not eaten breakfast, except for old man Robinson's coffee with goatmilk. He was in fact very hungry. "Kid, you want some beef jerky?"

"Thanks, but no thanks. I made myself some breakfast just before you showed up."

Foster walked on.

"So if you're hungry, what's that say about you?"

"That I'm tired of beef jerky."

The boy glanced up at him. "Okay. But you still get hungry."

"Kid, maybe we ought to walk down there." He pointed to a small ravine that eased down between two hills and wound toward the road gathering stands of grey brush and the occasional tree. “Get over the barbed wire and build a fire and cook some oatmeal.”

“I’d like that a lot. I like fires.”

They walked on down the hill. The boy went down on his belly and slid under the barbed wire fence and began gathering sticks as Foster found a sag in the wire, pushed it down and stepped over. They walked over to slabs of limestone that had been left bare by the cutting of storm waters next to the ravine.

The boy knew what he was doing. He broke off thin sticks and pulled up a wad of fine dry grass and brought them to Foster, then went for larger sticks. Foster dropped his backpack, unzipped it, and brought out the light aluminum pan he used for boiling water. He took off the lid and extracted two aluminum dishes that fit into the cooking pan, then began to lay the fire near the rock.

Before long, he took his canister of water and poured it all into the small pot. The boy delivered an armful of larger sticks, and Foster took his lighter and started the dry grass and twigs. Within a few minutes, the small fire was burning. He took two slabs of broken off limestone and built a platform next to the fire so he could place the pot over the fire. In a few minutes he had the water boiling.

The boy was sitting off to the side on a limestone rock watching the fire. Then he got up and moved nearer the fire, sat down, and held his hands toward the flames.

Foster added a little salt to the water, shook in some dried oatmeal from the cardboard cylinder, and then stirred it and waited.

It wasn’t long before he was scooping out thick, hot oatmeal with a tablespoon he carried into the two aluminum dishes. He handed the boy a mound of cooked oatmeal in one of the dishes. “I forgot to ask old man Robinson for syrup or sugar, but I do have a can of condensed milk,” he told the boy.

“Just like in pioneer times,” the boy said. “This is great.”

Foster used an army can opener on the milk can and poured some on his oatmeal, then handed the can to the boy, who did the same. Foster handed the boy his fork, and the boy took a bite. “Not too bad,” he said.

Foster took the tablespoon and began eating.

“So what’s this tell you about us?” the boy asked.

“Back to the game? You don’t give up.”

“That’s the fun of it. It keeps going. It can last as long as you want it to.”

"It tells us we like to eat. . . . We need to eat."

"Yes!" the boy shouted, as if he'd won some kind of victory. "And that there's such a thing as food that satisfies our need."

"Not much of mystery there," said Foster.

"Maybe not, but there are other things we all want too, and we want them because they are real," the boy said.

Foster took another bite and swallowed. "You're not going to start talking to me about sex, are you, kid?"

The boy's head jerked up. "Well, no." He was clearly embarrassed. "No," he said. "I was going to say that every tribe that people have found have some kind of religion. I was reading that famous book by a historian guy named Francis Parkman. The book's *The Oregon Trail.* He was living with the Sioux Indians up in the mountains way out west of here and was out hiking once and saw this Indian he knew from the village up there on the side of a mountain sitting all by himself and watching a pine tree blow in the wind. Parkman was sure the Indian was praying. That didn't surprise Parkman, because he knew these people were very religious—like all people."

"I know lots of people who aren't religious."

"That's the weird thing about these days," the boy said, eating his oatmeal. After a minute, he put down his fork and plate in the grass. "People say they aren't religious but pretty soon they're burning sage in their homes like praying Indians or burying statues in their yard when they want to sell their house or studying up on cooking or something or watching all kinds of sports and making sports their religion. They'll get all wrapped up in politics or something they're really interested in and treat it like a religion."

"You've seen that?"

"I have uncles and aunts and neighbors."

"What was old man Robinson's religion?"

The boy picked up his dish and ate another forkfull of oatmeal and milk. "I'd say it was his farm. He read up on all kinds of stuff, started raising goats, had a vegetable garden, tried different fertilizers on his crops. It was all he could talk about."

"And how has that turned out for him?—to quote a phrase I've heard recently."

The boy pulled the handkerchief from his coat pocket and wiped his mouth. "It hasn't turned out so good for Mr. Robinson. He can't farm much anymore and goats don't make very good gods."

"So some gods are better than others?" Foster was eating the last of his oatmeal.

"Back to the main question," the boy said.

"Which was? I've lost track." Foster put a glove on his hand and took the pot from the fire and shook out and spooned the rest of the oatmeal into the grass.

"The main question is why are people naturally religious?"

"Because we have to believe in something?" Foster said.

The boy, sitting on the rock, looked at Foster. "You really are good at this game! And if we're all hungry to believe in something, there must be something to believe in, something that makes us know that we've really found what we're hungry for." He took another bite, chewed, and swallowed. "Think about it. That French guy said that nobody regrets not having two mouths, but everybody would regret not having two eyes. And nobody wants three eyes. So when we all want something, want the same kind of thing all over the world, there must be something out there that satisfies us, or, like the animals, we wouldn't want it."

"Like sports," said Foster.

"But sports are so temporary. A football game is over in three hours. Even I can see that."

Foster took some dry grass and more or less cleaned his plate, picked up the boy's empty plate and cleaned it, poured a little water from his extra canteen and cleaned the pot, then put the plates back into the pot, snapped on the lid, then dropped it back into his backpack. "But it does it for you."

"Sports?"

"You make everything into a game. That's your religion."

The boy looked into the fire and held his hands out to the coals. "I like this game because it makes me think about big things. When the Kansas City Chiefs lose a game, I do get depressed, but it's not like life is over or anything. When I was ten, I cried when they lost a playoff game, but now I know, at least in my head, that it's not all that important. Like Plato said, you have to focus on the important things."

"Like being gods."

"Yes. Or kings."

"I've never been a king, kid."

"But you know you can be wretched," the boy said. "And that's proof you are great. He says our greatness is like the greatness of a broken king who lost his kingdom and somehow knows he needs to get it back."

Foster picked up his backpack and shouldered the straps. "I was never a king, kid."

"Then why are you out walking around without knowing where you're going?"

"Maybe because sports stopped doing it for me a long time ago, and work doesn't do it for me anymore."

"Do what for you?" The boy looked up.

Foster looked down at the boy sitting cross legged before the fire, still warming his hands with the coals, his big eyes on Foster. Foster just shook his head, and the boy looked down at his hands. "Thanks for the oatmeal and milk," he said. He rubbed his hands together, then stood up, slid his hands into his jean pockets and started stomping out the fire.

After stomping the coals into dirt, they walked back to the barbed wire fence. The boy rolled under as before and Foster shoved the top wire down and stepped over. Foster's hands slid into his own jeans pockets as he stepped onto the road. He felt the quarter he had saved for Jessica and pulled it out. "Have you seen these quarters, kid?" He showed him the Idaho state quarter with its image of a falcon.

"Yeah," the boy said, "I've seen some of the state quarters."

"I've got a game going with my daughter where we collect these. Trying to get all fifty states' quarters."

"Wow. I really like that. Maybe I should start doing that. Course, my mom will add her homeschooling rules if she knows about it."

"Well, don't tell her about it."

"We always work together on these things."

"Why rules?"

"Every game has rules."

"The only rule I came up with was you couldn't go to a bank and trade cash for a bag of quarters. What rules would your mom come up with?"

"Oh, she'll sure say that I've got to learn something about every state. Like the state capitol, the state bird, where it's located on the map. She'll make a list."

"Bummer," Foster said. "Sounds too much like work."

"Well, I can talk to her about it. She's reasonable. Like I'd love to find out some big historical event that happened in each state. I could tell her, 'Mom, I don't think I've got a chance of remembering every single state bird or flower even if I do memorize them. How about famous battles?' I think she might go for that." He started kicking a piece of gravel up the road. “I don’t mind rules,” the boy said. “It makes the game more challenging, don’t you think?”

“I expect you’re right, kid. You want this quarter to start your game?” He held it out.

They were walking over the concrete culvert that crossed the dry ravine. The boy shoved his hands into his jeans and said, “No, I think you should let your daughter have it. It was a game for her, wasn’t it?”

A large flock of blackbirds burst suddenly out of the pasture beyond the brush that bordered the ravine. They swerved into the sky. Hundreds of them turned together, rose again, and whirled in a twisting, soaring airborne river of fluttering, flashing black particles across the blue sky, then the stream of birds swerved upon itself, intersecting and descending till they settled back into the prairie grasses and disappeared.

“Do you think they have fun doing that?” the boy asked.

“Maybe. They’re good at it. I’ve seen huge flocks do that this time of year. A hawk was diving through them and couldn’t catch even one,” Foster said. “Kid, you can have the quarter. It’s got a hawk on it. I’ll find another quarter for my daughter. Maybe this one will start you on another game.”

The boy smiled and took the quarter. He examined the smooth image of the falcon as they walked, then slipped it into his pocket. The road rose gently toward a gravel crossroad.

The boy said, “I can’t go past the crossroad.”

“Why not?”

“My mom doesn’t let me go past that. It’s almost a mile from our house and my mom needs to be able to find me if she needs me.”

“She doesn’t let you have a phone?”

“There’s a phone in the house. I usually call her and tell her where I’m going, but I didn’t this time because I was in a hurry.”

“All right, kid. I’ll be seeing you around.”

They walked on a few paces, and the boy said, “I doubt that.”

Foster looked down at the baseball cap moving along near his elbow.

They came to the crossroad.

The boy stopped and Foster walked on. The white road ran on to the west, rising then dipping out of sight and reappearing more narrowly on the next rise, falling and rising toward a far horizon. He assumed the boy had turned for home, but when he glanced back, he saw him still standing there watching him: tan jacket, baseball cap, hands deep in his jean pockets.

Foster turned and raised his hand.

The boy's hand came quickly from his pocket and waved. Even from fifty yards, Foster could see him smile. The boy turned and ran for home.

"A good kid," Foster said as he turned to leave. "Smart, lonely, and happy all at the same time." The backpack weighed on his shoulders, his feet were still sore. He noticed that he was still walking west toward Cawker City and its massive ball of twine.

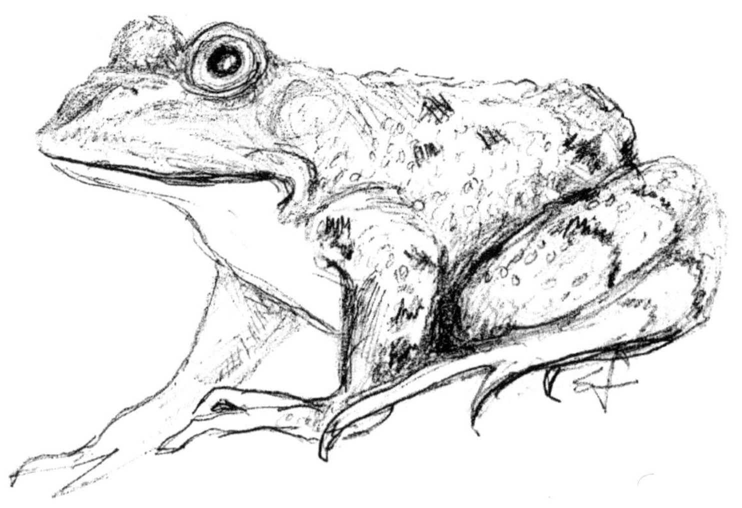

Amphibian

Stinging rain. Cold north wind. He saw himself passing in the plate glass windows of an antique shop, a hunched, dark green figure beneath a wet backpack, his gloved thumbs thrust beneath the shoulder straps, his head bent so the brim of his slumping camper's hat would keep the freezing rain from his eyes. He moved past an abandoned shop, came to a stoplight, crossed the street and turned north to face the biting wind. He waited for the light, but there was no traffic, so he moved across the street and passed the corner building: Jhett's Pizza. Closed.

He had been counting on finding a diner or a cafe. He pushed on past another abandoned store with paper sheeting shutting out the windows. He moved past a boutique with a manikin in a white dress, past a store called The Gossip, then past the office of Rural Water District #3. *Just what I need*, he thought, *more water*. His wet legs were numb with the cold, the rain beaded from his six-day-old scruff of a beard.

Then a shop with an OPEN sign appeared. Mare's Coffee Shop. *Mare's. A female horse? Was it pronounced Mary's*? The front glass pictured a green frog sipping from a white cup of coffee.

He pulled open the glass door. A little bell tinkled. He stepped in and felt the warmth of the place on his face.

A long narrow shop with high ceilings. Tables and chairs were scattered along the lefthand wall, a counter and coffee machines on the right, but no customers. It was about 9:30 in the morning and he assumed the breakfast rush, if there were one in such a small town as Holton, had already left for school or work. There was a large double door open in the lefthand wall that led into another long room with bookcases and more tables and chairs. No one there either, so he stepped into that room and found a table where he could still watch the counter and see the front door.

He unshouldered his muddy backpack and let it slump to the floor beside a chair, pulled off his wet gloves and laid them on the table. He rubbed his wet, freezing fingers together, took off his rumpled hat and laid it on the gloves, took off his rain jacket and draped it on the back of an adjacent chair. His fingers ached. On the wall of this second room he noticed an eight-foot-tall painting of a large lazy frog relaxing inside a cup of warm coffee. The yellowish-orange frog was taking a sauna bath, its front feet draped languidly over the coffee cup rim, its eyes blissfully half closed.

Foster Ulysses Turner was in no mood to smile. After six days hiking rural roads and a two-hour hike through freezing rain this morning, he was exhausted, hungry, angry that he had put himself here. Across from that warm, sleepy frog another large canvas depicted three more frogs sitting on mushroom stools around a mushroom table. They were playing cards, drinking frosty glasses of beer. One was smoking a pipe.

Amphibians, he thought, *the camaraderie of middle-class amphibians.*

He would have called for an Uber, but he had purposefully left his phone in his car six days ago. He had hidden that car in dried reeds a stone's throw from the Missouri River so that he could *not* check his work emails, social media, or call anyone. He had needed time away. Away from work. Away from family. Away from interruptions. Almost thirty years ago in high school, he had taken week-long hikes in the Blue Ridge Mountains of Virginia, camping out along mountain streams to escape the conflicts of school and home. In those days he had always hiked with a friend from school or with his little brother, but now he was alone and he felt it.

Three hours ago he had awakened in predawn darkness to wind shaking his tent and rain pelting down. His flashlight batteries had run down, so he had groped about in the dark of his tent, blindly rolling up his sleeping bag, stuffing it somehow into its dry sack, and that into his backpack. He had unzipped the tent door and shoved the pack out of the tent and had emerged like some unlikely amphibian into a rain-shaken greying dawn. After jerking up the tent stakes, he had rolled the tent and its fly tight, and attached them to his backpack. Already his gloves and knees were soaked by the relentless rain. He had hoisted the pack to his shoulders and stumbled out of the bare little grove of trees and brush he had camped beneath and set off up the muddy road through the blowing rain toward the town he knew was five or six miles away: *a ten-minute drive in my car, you damn fool,* he kept telling himself, but a two-hour trudge on mud and gravel farm roads up hill and down, dodging into grassy ditches when a car or pickup approached slashing icy water onto his jeans. Once he had slipped on ditch mud and gone down hard on his side, soaking half his body in ditch water. Cursing and yelling at the sky, he had pulled himself to his feet, reshouldered his backpack, deciding that if the town of Holton had a motel of any kind, he would stop this useless journey into nowhere, take a hot shower, wash his clothes, and hire a ride back to his car. Enough of this winter getaway.

He turned and walked back to the counter. The barista stood up from a stool where she had been paging through a book. She was a young woman with long dark hair and clear, grey eyes. She waited for his order.

"I need a large, hot, Americano coffee with three shots of espresso," he said.

She smiled, typed in the order, and went to work.

He walked back to his table and sat down on his hands. His soaked, muddy jeans had a cold grip on his thighs and he clenched his teeth trying to suppress the shiver running through his bones. He looked out a plate glass window streaked with rain. Across the street in the center of the old-fashioned city square, stood a pale, blocky county courthouse with a flat roof. Not beautiful. Bare limbs of a grey tree were bending and straining in the wind. No one was out walking on this miserable December morning.

He listened to the hiss and squawk of the espresso machine and pushed his hands further beneath his thighs. Acid thoughts. What a fool he was. What a damned, fucking fool.

He recalled a day in late summer when he and his younger brother had taken their little sailboat on a three-day journey down the Chesapeake Bay. They had loved that little boat, having both saved up hard-earned money to buy it from a neighbor. Foster had named it *Shark*, but his more reasonable little brother had called it *Tadpole*. They had camped out at random along shore and fished in the evenings. But on the second day the wind had died when they were a mile from shore and the rudder was useless without wind. He remembered his frustration as the boat swung this way and that. He kept cursing and ducking as the sail's boom swung over their heads as the boat drifted. His young brother had laughed: "Tie down the boom, Foster, so it doesn't decapitate us." Then his always even-tempered brother had taken his fishing pole and made the best of their circumstances, catching three fish during four hours of calm as Foster's temper simmered and burned. A hot summer afternoon. Still and humid. He had put his head back on a life preserver and tried to sleep, but his brother's shouts when he caught a fish kept waking him. Finally, a slight evening breeze had passed over his sweating face. The sail filled and allowed them to finally make shore where his brother filleted the three fish and fried them up. It had turned out to be a wonderful evening, but ten years ago his brother had married a girl from England and had moved across the Atlantic. They rarely communicated these days.

After a couple of minutes, the barista placed the big ceramic mug on the counter and looked over at him. "Cream? Sugar?"

"No." He stood stiffly to his feet and hobbled over to the counter. His wet feet were sore and cold from the six days of endless walking with little to think about but his unhappy wife and angry thirteen-year-old daughter back in Kansas City. He used to think himself a decent husband and father, but over the last two years, he had lost interest in his work and had begun to avoid his wife and daughter. He wasn't sure why. He didn't intend to alienate them, but his growing dissatisfaction depressed him and he resented answering his wife's questions about his change in temperament.

For years he had lost himself in that strangely engrossing business of simply being busy. He was a talented graphic designer and he knew it, but gradually his love of art and design, even the satisfaction of being paid larger and larger sums for his work had lost any sense of fulfillment. He had spent long minutes in his office staring beyond his computer at the passing traffic on the avenue below his office. An endless rushing river of steel running in opposite directions.

Fall had come with its brightening maples, yellow cottonwoods, and brown-leaved oaks in the nearby park, but his motivation to accomplish good work and please his customers had drained away and he had begun shifting his anger onto those customers. He stopped playing handball and going to a favorite bar with two longtime friends. He told his wife to go out to eat with her friends while he stayed home and read books: Russian novels and a travel book that led him deep into Siberia. His young teenaged daughter noticed his fading presence and tried to get him to watch television with her. Instead, he bought her a video game.

Now, standing at the counter, he withdrew his wet, leather billfold and opened it. The billfold pocket, as he knew, was empty. He had spent his last five-dollar bill at a small gas station the day before in Denison, an even smaller country town. He was about to extract one of his several credit cards, but stopped and showed the girl the empty wallet. He was angry and wanted to see her reaction.

Her grey eyes opened wider. "You don't have any money?"

He shrugged.

"Are you homeless?"

He shrugged.

She glanced at the door, then at the back of the café. "Have you eaten?"

He shook his head no.

"Are you hungry?"

"Famished."

She went to work. She pulled out a ciabatta bun, sliced it in two and dropped the two halves in a big toaster. "You like ham and cheese?" she asked without looking up.

"Sure."

She opened a stainless steel container, took a pair of tongs and pulled out several slices of ham and two or three slices of American cheese. When the toast popped, she put it all together, slathered on some mayonnaise, and placed it on a plate. "You want a cinnamon roll?"

"Sure."

"You want it heated up?"

"Of course."

She nodded, took the tongs and extracted a cinnamon roll from beneath a glass counter, placed it on a small plate, heated it in the microwave and set it all on the counter next to the large cup of coffee.

"Who's paying?" he asked.

"Me." She glanced up, but those clear grey eyes didn't smile.

"Or the café?" he asked.

"No, me." She reached for the jar of tips, emptied it and he watched her count out six dollars and fifty cents, then reach below the counter for a small purse and count out the rest. "Plus the coffee," she said, pulling out another five-dollar bill from her purse and putting it in the cash register.

"You going to give yourself a tip?" he asked.

She didn't smile at his lame joke.

"Why would you pay for this?" Foster asked.

She gave him a quizzical look. "You're hungry you said . . . and you're cold."

He took the plate with its sandwich and cinnamon roll, the brown mug of coffee and walked into the second room with its sleepy frog. He sat down, cupping his hands around the hot cup and sipped at his Americano. He hated the fact that his little deception had cost the girl over twenty dollars, but he was still angry and now he was embarrassed to admit he had several credit cards in another pocket of his billfold.

He wondered if his often angry thirteen-year-old daughter would ever find it in her heart to pay for a homeless man's meal. His wife would have paid without a second thought. She was a fulltime nurse and her personality leaned into sympathetic service, which made her alienation from Foster harder for both to bear. She had recently moved out, taking their daughter Jessica with her. Before leaving, he again remembered her crying out, "Find something, Foster! Find someone, do something to get yourself together! I can't stand to be around you anymore, neither can Jessica!"

He hadn't told his wife or his daughter that he was leaving town for a week or two.

Now he picked up the sandwich and consumed it. He rubbed his aching fingers together and bit into the warm cinnamon roll. Delicious. He kept sipping at his coffee. It was very good. His hands were warming, but the coffee was beginning to cool, the warmth evaporating.

It was still spitting rain outside. No one coming in for coffee or sandwiches. The girl sitting behind the counter was idly paging through a book. Looking past the satisfied frog, he again noticed one of the bookcases. He wanted to wait out the rain and warm up, but now he couldn't ask the girl for a second cup of coffee, nor could he ask her if there was a motel in the area without making her wonder where he'd get the money to pay for it. He sure as hell wouldn't let her pay for his motel. Maybe he could justify his presence by reading a book.

He got up and checked a few book titles: popular thrillers, romances, nothing he was interested in. No Russian novels. He wasn't sure why he liked Russian authors. Maybe because their books were complicated and serious, filled with characters and conflicts that extracted him from his blasé life in Kansas City. After his wife and daughter left him, he had found that if he wasn't reading, his mind would automatically return to three or four of his latest designs for customers and he would be lost in a warren of alternative passageways: possible shades of color, new images, distinctive letterings. However successful his business had become, and it had been very successful, he had tired of the constant pull to design and redesign and design again.

He had recently read *Dr. Zhivago* by Pasternak. He had chosen the novel because he had loved the movie in spite of its sad ending, but the novel itself was far more depressing than the movie, with a protagonist who eventually wanders into a meaningless maze of a life before dying of a heart attack. Strangely, after the novel's ending, the book continued with a collection of the main character's poems, some of them religious, which Foster knew was unusual in atheistic Soviet Union, but Russians loved their poets. He didn't know what to make of the poems. Maybe they lost something in translation.

In this bookcase of used books before him he found no Tolstoy, no Dostoevsky, Gogol, Solzhenitsyn, not even Chekhov. He thought of the book he had been reading when he left home: Isaac Babel's diary of his months riding with the Red Cavalry in their wretched little war with Poland in the years following the Russian Revolution. Babel's record of exhaustion, mud, rain, the butchering of prisoners, demoralizing retreats, black night journeys in the baggage train, absolute exhaustion and inability to sleep seemed strangely the right read for his present journey. Yet it had occurred to him while reading quietly in his Kansas City apartment that he was in fact a very, very fortunate man: a wife he still believed liked him, a daughter who wanted to spend time with him at least occasionally, a growing business, a warm, secure apartment, plenty of money, friends when he wished. Why this present desolation?

Isaac Babel, Pasternak, Solzhenitsyn had had little choice. War had ripped away the ancient culture and expectations of tsarist Russia. New ideologies were storming their world with blizzard force. Revolution could inspire a young man with new hopes, but in his Red Cavalry stories, Babel described the Cossacks he was riding with as brutal men: cursing and raping and killing, the nurses sleeping with all the officers, the men beating and killing an old Jewish man, dead Poles lying bloated in a wheat field, their faces slashed, artillery bombardments pounding into them, more rain. And here was Foster, alone in his apartment, relaxing on a leather armchair, sipping bourbon, and reading a book about far away and long ago . . . Why now this winter of discontent?

As he stood beside the bookcase, he looked through the doorway at the girl. She glanced up at him. He nodded at her.

"Do you like to read?" she asked.

"Yes I do, but how much are these books?"

"They're used books so they're only ten dollars each, but you can read one and put it back when you're ready to go. Do you want more coffee? The rain is going to change to snow this morning. You might want to warm up for a while."

He opened his mouth to thank her, but at that moment someone pulled open the front door, jingling its bell. From his angle at the bookcase, he could see the front door. A middle-aged woman in a grey winter coat closed her black umbrella and stood it against the wall. "My God, what a day out there!" she cried. She walked to the counter. "How are you, Cindy? Must be a bad day for business. No tips, I see."

The barista smiled. "Having the usual this morning, Dorothy?"

"Absolutely!"

Dorothy turned from the counter and noticed Foster paging through a book from the bookcase. "Great day for hot coffee and a good book, isn't it?" she asked him.

Foster looked up from across the room and forced a smile.

"What cha reading?" the woman asked.

Foster looked at the book he had pulled out at random. "Looks like *Heart of Darkness*," he said, reading the cover title.

"Oh! Oh! I read that in college, I think. Wasn't that Orwell?"

Foster held up the book, showing her the cover. "Joseph Conrad, apparently."

"Conrad? Conrad. Well, maybe I didn't read it."

Foster smiled. "Well," he said, "I don't remember much of what I read in college either."

"Isn't that the truth," she said. "We spend all that money on college and whoof! Out the ears it all flies. What did Orwell write anyway? I know I read him in my lit class, or maybe it was Western Civ."

Foster was paging through *Heart of Darkness.* He glanced up at the lady. "*Nineteen Eighty-Four* was it? I once read his *Down and Out in Paris and London*." He noticed that Cindy the barista was listening to their exchange as she squirted flavoring into Dorothy's coffee.

"*Nineteen Eighty-Four*! That's it! I did read that. What a depressing book! Never again. I remember telling my girlfriends, never again! I shouldn't have to buy a novel just to add to my depression and then have to wade through it every day in class. What's the point? What *is* the point?"

Cindy set the hot drink on the counter. "Here's your latte, Dorothy."

The woman paid for her drink, put a dollar in the tip jar, took a tentative sip, and glanced out the plate-glass window. "Oh, my goodness, would you look at that? Snow! I swear it's all turning to snow. Big old wet flakes!" She smiled brightly at Foster, and walked to the front door, picked up her umbrella, pushed open the door, and stepped out, trying to hold her drink with one hand while opening the umbrella with the other.

Cindy waved to her, then turned to Foster. "Here, I forgot to get your coffee. Another Americano?"

Foster was embarrassed. "No, no. Just coffee. You can use this cup." He walked over and handed her the empty ceramic cup.

"You've read Orwell?" she asked as she turned to pour his coffee. "What was that book you mentioned? By Orwell?"

"*Down and Out in Paris and London*? It's not a novel; it's an account of Orwell living with the lower working class in Paris. He was a dishwasher. Lived in a horrid apartment infested with bedbugs by the thousands. Later he joined tramps wandering from place to place in England. The government wouldn't let them spend more than one night in any one place if they were vagrants. I think Orwell wanted to see what that lifestyle was like. It's an interesting book."

"Is that why you're out hiking in this weather?" she asked. "You don't sound like a homeless guy." She set the steaming cup on the counter and he walked over to pick it up.

"You like to read?" he said.

She held up a paperback book and said, "*The Way It Is*, by William Stafford. It's poetry. My aunt sent me the book. She lives in Hutchinson, Kansas where Stafford was born."

"Never liked poetry much," he said.

"You have to take it slow," she said. "Like sipping whisky." She smiled. "It's concentrated language, distilled. That's what Aunt Mildred says."

"Maybe I should try it," he said. "I like a slow glass of bourbon. You should read me a line or two." He took a sip of his new cup of coffee and felt the warmth in his hands.

She looked down, brushing back a strand of long dark hair behind an ear. "Okay. It's kind of a sad poem." She read: "In the maples an insect sang/ insane for hours about how deep the dark was." She looked up.

He shrugged.

She ran her finger down the page and read, "When I went back I saw many sharp things:/ the wild hills coming to drink at the river,/ the church pondering its old meanings." She looked up and shrugged her shoulders. "You have to give it time."

"What's the title of the poem?"

"Back Home," she read.

"In Kansas?"

"It sounds like it. A girl sings in the church choir but ends up—here, I'll read it. 'the girl who used to sing in the choir/ broke into jagged purple glass.'"

"Not a happy poem."

She held up the book and showed him the title again: *The Way It Is.*

Someone pulled open the glass door. A large, middle-aged man with a wide smile. He took off his farmer's cap and shook it. "Freezing out there!" he announced. "Snow again." Grey-silver hair matted a head that seemed thrust into his broad shoulders. He had on a canvas coat.

Cindy said, "Otis! You've got a hole in your knee."

"That I do, Cindy. Slipped on some snow just up the street. Ripped a hole in my jeans. Or jean. Why do they call them jeans, or pants . . . or slacks. It's one shirt, a pair of socks I can understand, but only one pant, isn't it? With a pair of legs."

"Maybe," Cindy smiled, "maybe it's because they want to charge you twice as much for a pair of jeans than just one jean."

"That's it, Cindy! You're a genius. First person I ever met who knew the answer to that. Speaking of money" He walked over to the counter. "You ever run into Leroy Jenkins? Plumber. He's a plumber, and a good one. Had him do some work in our basement a couple of years ago. Leroy had a place out in the country, south of here near the Potawatomie reservation."

"I don't remember the name," she said.

"Well, he made a decent living. Then he did all the plumbing for a big new stone house out near Seneca. Fell in love with that place. Used to tell his wife if he had a place like that he'd never complain about anything again. Well, wouldn't you know it, some aunt of his died and left him over a million bucks. I'm not lying! A million dollars. He got the plans to that same house he had worked on and had it built on his own land. Cost him all of that million and more, even though he did his own plumbing. So he had his American dream right there under his own two feet on the little farm he grew up on. They moved in and started living in it, but found out they couldn't afford the taxes and insurance on the new place. He had to sell it at a big loss cause nobody wanted a mansion on his grubby little farm way out in the country. So he had to move to a little two-bedroom place there in Seneca to keep from going broke. What do you think of that?"

Cindy shook her head. "I'm sorry to hear that."

"Well, I am too, but at least he's got a place to warm his toes in weather like this."

"What can I get for you, Otis?"

"Make it a big hot mocha today. I got to sweeten up my disposition after ruining my one jean here."

"Paper cup?"

"Yep. I need to drive home and change before gettin' back to work. Can't linger and sip today."

He turned to survey the shop while waiting and noticed Foster sipping his coffee at a table and reading a book. He saw Foster's backpack and hat. "You been out in this?"

Foster looked up and nodded.

"Hiking in this kind of weather?"

Foster shrugged.

"Where you headed? You can't be out walkin' in this today. I hear it's going to blow hard this afternoon."

Foster shrugged.

"Well, you just can't. I'll take you on over to Motel 8 and get you a place to sit this out."

Foster didn't want to admit he had money and these talkative small-town people were annoying him. He pulled out his billfold and showed Otis the empty pocket.

"Well, that ain't no excuse," the big man said. "We can't have a man out traipsing around in a Kansas blizzard. You come on over to my place and hole up there for the night. You can get a change of clothes, maybe take a nice hot shower. My wife's at work and might get home before I finish up at the meat plant, but I'll give her a call so she don't walk in on you and have a heart attack when she sees a strange man sittin' at her dining room table."

Foster didn't like this. He wanted to pay for his motel room and spend the night alone, but again, he was ashamed to have deceived Cindy, so he took a deep breath and said, "All right. I appreciate it. I hope it's not too much trouble."

Cindy gave Otis his hot mocha, he paid, left her a dollar bill in the glass jar, and turned back to Foster. "Come on now," he said, "we got to get you warmed up. Watch the sidewalk out there; she's slippery."

Foster lifted his backpack, placed his hat on his head and grabbed the gloves. He took a last sip of his coffee and looked at Cindy. "I'll be getting some money soon. I'll pay you back."

She looked at him and shrugged. He knew she didn't believe a broke homeless man would ever return, but she smiled and nodded as he followed Otis to the door.

The big man zipped up his canvas coat, put his cap back on his head, and held the door for Foster. The wind was driving the wet snow horizontally and Foster grabbed at his cap before it could fly off his head. He followed big Otis to a grey double-cab Ford pickup. The wind cut through his wet jeans.

Otis opened the back door so Foster could shove his backpack in, then motioned him around to the front seat.

They both climbed in and Otis took a sip of his mocha and started the pickup. "Mercy!" he said. "You sure picked a helluva time of year to be out hiking. Here, let me turn up the heat."

Foster didn't respond.

"Where you from?" He backed the truck into the street and turned toward home.

Foster was shaken by the man's generosity. It didn't sit easily with his desire for isolation. He had gradually, over the last two years, abandoned camaraderie. He looked at big Otis and answered his question: "I've been living in Kansas City. You help strangers often?"

Otis's big shoulders hunched a little more as he drove from the city square and soon into the blowing countryside. The wet flakes had suddenly turned to sleet; the tiny pits of ice rattled on the side of the truck. "No, not that many opportunities these days to help out a man who I don't know, but you got to deal with reality and reality today says you can't let a man with no money walk this weather."

"I've got money, just not on me."

Otis adjusted the brim of his farmer's cap and glanced at him. "You homeless or something?"

"For now I am."

Sleet was skipping across the wet asphalt and collecting in the grassy ditches and blowing down the furrows of cut-down corn stalks. A few black Angus cows stood in a pasture, their tails to the wind. Foster remembered walking by that very field earlier, remembered how very long it had taken just to walk that one fence line. He had counted the posts: four steel posts, then a wooden post made of a tree limb, four steel posts, then a tree limb, four . . . .

"Well," Otis interrupted his thoughts, "let me pull into my house on up here a ways and change my jeans. I'll leave you off. You can get yourself a shower and warm up. Make yourself a meal. I'll give the wife a call and we'll both see you around five."

After driving several miles more, he turned into a long driveway that led to a brick single-story with a metal barn near it. His driveway took him between the two buildings and around behind his home. A three-sided lean-to shed stood behind a fence. As he pulled up near the back door of his home, Foster could see a large Hereford bull standing in the shed and a smaller cow beside it.

"You raise cattle?" Foster asked.

"Oh no. Oh no, no. I *wanted* to raise cattle. I surely did. But there's a difference between wanting and doing. Bought Abraham there to get the herd going. My wife who's a church-going woman said the name Abraham means Father of Nations, so I was all for that. Get me a nation of Herefords and maybe in time I'd start on Angus cows too. I got 40 acres of pasture and a creek and need to sell cows to pay my taxes on the property, maybe make a little once the herd gets going. Cost me over 4000 bucks for that beast. Then picked up little Sarah there for just under a thousand and told 'em to get busy having them some kids." He parked the truck and turned off the engine. He sipped at his mocha.

The Hereford bull's white face turned and observed them from beneath the shed roof. The cow stood near it, their reddish hair almost black in the shadows, the sleet pelting the galvanized roof of the shed.

"Young Abraham here and Sarah ain't had a calf now in three years. Just like in the good book, Sarah's barren as a rock post. So I had to buy me a second cow. The wife called her Hagar and she had a calf a year ago, but I cracked an elbow slipping on cow shit while helping a friend unload sacks of fertilizer and was out of work for some time, so we had to sell Hagar and her calf to make ends meet last year. So I don't have any big hopes that young Abraham and Sarah are going to get the job done."

He opened the cab door. "Come on in now and get yourself warmed up. I got to change clothes and get back to work."

Foster retrieved his backpack and followed Otis to the back door of the house. Otis pulled out his keys, opened the door and held it for Foster. They passed through a little mud room that held rubber boots, rakes and shovels standing against the wall. He opened the inside door to his living room and ushered Foster in.

Foster stepped in just as a woman with an apron walked out of their kitchen and stopped.

Otis stepped in. "Nasty! What you doin' home today?"

The woman glared at Otis. "Otie, what did I tell you? Never call me that in front of guests." She spoke with an accent of some kind. She looked at Foster. "My name is Anastasia. He just loves embarrassing me."

Otis laughed. "Sorry, Dear. Sorry. You caught me by surprise there." He took off his canvas coat and hung it near the back door. "I met this lady here in Germany when I was in the service. It's an unusual name in these parts. She's from Slovakia of all places. See, she's got her picture icons all over the walls."

Foster glanced around. It was a large living room with a cathedral ceiling and a reddish brick fireplace on the right with a large television screen above the wooden mantle. Across the room there were two watercolor paintings near the front door: pale landscapes of Kansas hills. Next to the back door where they'd entered, an icon of the Virgin and Child hung above a small shelf. "I see one icon," Foster said.

"Oh, she's got 'em in every room. Anyway, why *are* you home, Stasia? I thought you had to work today." He took off his cap and hung it with his coat. Then he pointed at his knee. "Busted a hole in my knee, Stasia. Got to change quick and get back to work. What is it, 10:30 in the morning already?"

She glanced at the hole in his jeans. "Did you hurt yourself?"

"Aw, nah. Little scrape is all. I'll throw a little iodine on it and slap on a bandaid."

She looked at Foster who had placed his backpack on the floor near the back door.

"Hang your jacket up next to Otie's coat," she said, then, to Otis: "Barb called me on my way to work and said a blizzard's coming and she was cancelling all the afternoon appointments and said I ought to stay home and not fight the storm. So I turned around and came back. Put the Chevy in the garage. Thought I'd bake you some bread and surprise you when you got home."

"Oh, I do love me some home-baked bread."

Foster saw her glance at him and look back at Otis, waiting on him to explain the presence of a stranger with a backpack. "This here is . . ." He looked at Foster and hesitated.

"I'm Foster Turner."

"Guess we never got around to names," said Otis. "This man was out hiking in the rain. Got no place to hole up and a blizzard blowin' down out of Nebraska. Didn't expect you'd be here, Stace." He paused. "Anyway, I was going to leave him here and give you a call to let you know we had a guest while I run on back to work."

"Good. I'll bake the bread and get him warmed up."

Otis stood his ground and looked at Foster. "Well, Stasia, I got to get back to work and I'm not leavin' a man I don't know that well in my house with the wife. No offense Turner, but now that I think about it, it don't seem right."

Foster reached down and reshouldered his backpack.

"Otie, he's here," she said. "He needs a place. He looks pretty well soaked. The man needs to warm up."

"Motel 8's got hot showers last I heard. I ain't leavin' him here."

"It's blowing like crazy out there, Otie. Look at the sleet! Maybe you should call Charlie and see if he can let you off for the day. Nobody should be driving around in this weather. Next thing we know, you'll be slid off the road and I'll have to come pull you out myself."

"That means both of us ain't workin' today, Stace. That's an expense."

She stood there with her hands in her apron pocket. She was a stout woman with long blondish hair going grey at the roots and high Slavic cheekbones. She waited for his decision.

"Well, you win." He looked at Foster and added, "She most always wins." He grinned his wide smile. "I'll give Charlie a call. I expect he'll be sendin' everybody home before long anyhow."

Anastasia smiled and clapped the flour from her hands. "Good. Otie, why don't you show Mr. Turner to our spare bedroom and the shower. Have you got extra clothes in that backpack, Mr. Turner, or do you need to borrow some from Otie?"

Foster didn't like the situation. "Look, you don't need to do this."

"Well, yes we do," she said. "You're soaked. You must be freezing. Just dump your dirty clothes out right there next to the door and I'll start a load of laundry."

Foster looked at them both, he a tall, robust man, she, a shorter, handsome woman. "Look, I could call my wife in Kansas City and have her come get me. I hate for both of you to miss work on account of me."

"In this weather? You don't want your wife driving into the teeth of a Kansas blizzard. Why on earth did she let you go hiking in the middle of winter anyway? Even Otie here wouldn't get away with that."

Foster caught the big smile on Otis's face again. Foster dropped his backpack on the floor, reached down and clicked open the straps, unzipped the top and pulled out the big waterproof drybag where he had shoved his dirty clothes. "I think they're all in here."

"Well, you need to get out of those wet clothes. Otie, go get him a sweatshirt and pants while you're getting out of your own pants."

"Pant," he said.

"What?"

"Never mind." Otis motioned for Foster to follow him and they made their way back to their bedroom. He opened the door and Foster followed. On the wall above the big bed was a stuffed pheasant landing on a branch. On two walls were icons of ancient saints.

The bedroom faced the south. The driving sleet was collecting on the concrete driveway, a grainy crust of ice, but now the snow had returned, tiny flakes sweeping into the pale pasture grasses. Beyond the shed that sheltered Abraham and Sarah, the pasture sloped down toward a line of leafless trees that followed a stream. Beyond the tree line, the pasture rose through blowing snow toward an indistinct horizon. Wind was swirling the snow, fading the trees, a powder snow that Foster knew meant the temperature had plummeted.

He stood as Otis rummaged through a dresser drawer.

Foster looked again at the stuffed colorful bird above the bed. "You shoot that pheasant?" he asked.

Otis stood up. "Oh, sure. Love to pheasant hunt every fall. Got three of 'em this fall out near Hays. There's a few of them birds around here, but not enough to find 'em when you need 'em." He returned to the drawer, making a mess of the folded clothes but finally pulling out the needed sweatshirt and a red flannel shirt, pants, and two pairs of wool socks.

Foster was examining the icons. "Who is the old man?" he asked, looking at a gold-haloed saint with a severe face robed in white with black crosses.

Otis laid out the sweatshirt on the bed and looked up. "Oh, that's uncle Augie."

"Your uncle?" He smiled.

"No. The wife claims him, but I'm not much into all that."

Foster couldn't read the Cyrillic script next to the golden halo. "What language is that?"

"Oh, it's some kind of Russian. She brought that from Germany, says her dad loved his Saint Augustine, was named after the man, so she hung it up. Look, I'm going to use the master bath here to get cleaned up and patch up the knee, and I got to call Charlie, but the main bath is just down the hall to the left." He handed Foster the sweatshirt, sweatpants, and a pair of socks and said, "Take your time. Make it hot, or you're liable to catch a helluva chill after that morning jog of yours."

Foster found the bath and in it a glassed shower with an overhead shower head.

He peeled off his wet pants, socks, and underwear. He was still cold. In the hot, pouring stream of the shower he felt his entire body warm and relax. Steam filled the little bathroom. He stood, head bowed, recalling the blissful frog on the coffee shop wall. *From morning misery to sudden bliss,* he thought. *I'm a fortunate amphibian.*

By the time he returned to the living room with his wadded wet jeans, socks, and shirt, he could smell the baking bread. Otis, wearing a red flannel shirt now and sweat pants, had just brought in sticks and a number of split logs to build a fire in the brick fireplace. He was laying the sticks, shoving in some crumpled newspaper, and arranging the logs.

An hour later the fire was roaring and Foster and Otis were seated at the dining room table. The dining room, like the kitchen, opened onto the living room so that Foster could see the fire as Anastasia brought in a tureen of ham and bean soup. The baked bread had already been sliced and placed on the oak table. She sat down, crossed herself, and recited the prayer of thanksgiving in a language Foster didn't recognize. She stood and spooned out the lumpy, rich-smelling soup and passed the bowls.

It was as fine a lunch as Foster could remember. Otis had even opened three bottles of dark German beer. Foster wasn't particularly hungry, having wolfed down breakfast just two hours before, but Anastasia's soup was worth eating and the freshly baked and buttered bread was wonderful.

Anastasia began asking the normal questions about his family and work. He answered as best he could without revealing the fact that wife and daughter had moved out. She finally asked the obvious question: why had he left work and home to walk the Kansas hills in the middle of winter?

Foster was tired of the series of little deceptions that had carried his conversations that morning. He had always liked surprising people and amusing himself with their reactions, but why now this sudden need to lie? He put his soup spoon down, broke off a piece of bread, buttered it, and said, "Depression maybe? Arguments at home, no fun at work anymore. I don't know. No reason. No good reason at all. I just needed to get the hell out and walk."

He looked out the dining room window. Thick snow was swirling, collecting on the outside of this north-facing window and shutting out the winter landscape.

Otis saw him gazing out the window and said, "You're damn lucky to have made it to Holton before all this wind and snow buried you in some ditch. I knew a rancher once, walked out in a blizzard like this to his barn, no more than 40 yards, and got lost. His son found him dead the next day."

Foster looked at him and then at Anastasia who had stopped eating and was watching him intently. "What you said about depression," she said, "and home life *are* reasons. There are always reasons. Right reasons and wrong reasons. If we keep getting no answers, maybe we aren't asking the right question." She looked at her husband.

Otis frowned. "What? What are you looking at me for? Did I ask the wrong questions?"

She smiled and said, "Once at least you did ask the right question."

"When?"

"In Vilsek."

"In Germany?"

She looked at the fire across the room. "You asked if I loved you."

Otis sat back in his chair. "Well of course! Who wouldn't love this handsome soldier from the good old USA?"

"Then why did you ask?"

He looked at her and smiled his wide smile.

She looked out the window and sighed. "Well, we're glad you're here, Mr. Turner . . . and safe."

Foster began eating the bread and soup again. Questions. He remembered the boy two days ago walking with him up the dirt and gravel road on that cool, clear morning. The boy who had joined his walk for almost an hour and had made up question games. His first question had been, 'Are you walking away from something or toward something?' Foster had told the boy he didn't know, but the boy kept at his game.

Somehow, the question game had found its way to Plato the Philosopher saying something about play being more important than work, then on to some French mathematician's comments, something about understanding that human beings are walking brains, weak weeds with cabbage heads, he had said, that are, each one, greater than the physical universe. Absurd. How then, had he seemed to agree? It seemed a strange, twisted little game the boy was playing, but enjoyable at the time. The kid was getting a very different education than Foster had had in middle school. Foster remembered the boy had said that we are kings, but wretched because we know we're going to die. He remembered rejecting kingship but silently agreeing with the sense of wretchedness.

A gust of wind rattled the limbs of an overhanging tree against the roof.

Otis looked up. "Sounds like I need to clip some a them limbs. Must be weighed down with ice. This storm's liable to sock us in for a while."

Foster looked at these strangers quietly eating their food. He remembered that twenty-four hours before he had been trudging alone mile after mile. The teenager's crazy comments had annoyed him. Why would some ancient Greek have the authority or the wits to tell him that play was more important than work, for example. Then it had occurred to him a half mile later that taking an extended hike away from work just might qualify as recreation to some people and that the very word *recreation* seemed to identify exactly his present purpose: getting away from work, family, and friends to reorder if not recreate himself.

Otis finished his beer and asked Foster if he wanted another, but Foster put up his hand. "Can't hold any more. I had breakfast a couple hours ago, but this is excellent food. Excellent food. Thank you for taking me in."

Anastasia said, "You're very welcome." She got up, and started clearing the table. Otis stood up too and asked Foster if he was a fan of the Kansas City Chiefs. He told Otis he used to be, but had lost interest.

Big Otis stopped. "Just when we got a streak of going to the Super Bowls? What kind of fan are you?"

Foster scooted back his chair and stood up. "I must have a few screws loose. I know it doesn't make sense."

Otis walked over to the television, picked up the remote and clicked it on. "Have a seat here, Turner. We ain't goin' out in this weather for nobody nor nothin'. Here, let me hit the weather channel. See how long this storm's stayin' with us."

+ + +

The blizzard swept over the region for two long days, pushing snowbanks across the rural highways, shutting down all traffic.

Two or three hours after the sun set that first night, the electricity in Otis and Anastasia's house blinked out. Otis cursed and Anastasia got up to light candles. They had eaten a fine meal of roast beef, mashed potatoes, and asparagus by the time the lights went out, so again, Foster found himself thinking he was eating better in this place than in Kansas City restaurants which he had resorted to after his wife moved out.

Since lights and television were suddenly gone, Otis built up the fire in the fireplace and they fell into long conversations about Otis's work and Anastasia's job at the Eye doctor's, about Foster's graphic design business, about Otis and Anastasia's two daughters who had both married and moved out of state.

Foster had not made a new friend in several years, but he liked these two, as different as they were from each other: Otis was full of tales about local farmers, ranchers, workers; Anastasia talked of friends and family. Otis had worked at the local Johnsonville sausage and hot dog plant for almost 20 years; he was a machine mechanic and general fix-it man for the plant. Anastasia had worked a number of jobs, but had recently settled into working for the local optometrist. She liked the job because it gave her introductions to new friends and acquaintances in the area.

That first night, after a nightcap of Otis's favorite whisky, Foster slept alone in the guest bedroom. Lying there in the cooling bedroom, the blankets pulled to his chin, he thought of Cindy the barista, of the boy who loved games and books and talking to a stranger, of this couple who seemed to struggle with money but treated him like family.

He remembered the miles. Pacing down dirt roads under a pale winter sky. A sagging shed near the road filled with bald tires and rusted rims, a car jack. An abandoned two-story home of native limestone, roofless. There, he had walked through knee-high dried grasses to the burnt doorframe and looked at the collapsed floor inside. In one corner of the old basement lay a rusted freezer, in another a knee-high packrat nest of jumbled sticks scattered with wooden clothespins, black zip ties, chicken feathers, old beer cans, and plastic figures from an old game of chess. *Even the packrats,* he thought, *are good Americans, piling up their possessions, trying out zip ties, random clothespins, a new kind of beer, maybe chess tonight? then hiding beneath it all.*

On that last evening of bone-tired hiking, he had watched a distant cloudbank rising slowly in the west over sullen hills, shutting out the setting sun. The premature loss of sunlight had forced him into that grove of trees where he had hastily set up the tent, built his campfire and heated his last can of beef stew. The bagels he'd bought at the gas station in Denison were long gone. After eating the can of beef stew, he had still been hungry. *Which means,* he thought, *that there is in fact such a thing as food, but maybe not for damn fools who go hiking in midwinter.*

He needed to call Carol his wife. Why abandon a decent marriage? Why cut a wife and daughter loose because of his own dissatisfaction? Why not control his temper and moods? But he had tried and failed too many times to count.

The wind blew hard that first night. He awoke several times to the scrape and rattle of the limbs overhead. Increasing cold. Anastasia had left him extra blankets and he pulled one up and slept again.

By the second night the whole house seemed to be cocooned in snow that had covered the highway and banked high on the north side of the home. A great silence settled over the house. After their shots of whisky the second night, Otis didn't get up and go to bed, but poured them a second round. Anastasia turned hers down, but Foster sipped his and stared into the fire watching the logs burn down to red coals. By that time the whole house was cold. They had drawn their chairs closer to the fire and closer together. After a third round of whisky, Otis fell asleep in his chair, his big head on his chest.

Anastasia was wrapped in a sweatshirt and a housecoat, wool socks on her feet. She placed them nearer the coals, looked up and said, "You know it was a shock to me when Otie brought you here."

Foster looked up. "Shock?"

"When he brought me here from Germany, I was lonely. I'd always been a social girl. Lots of friends, boys and girls. Even adults. But here Otis kind of wanted to keep me here with him. I was still trying to get beyond the English I learned in Slovakia, so for a while I couldn't find a job. My only connections were in church. We had married in Germany in a Catholic church, so he knew me going to church was not up for debate. The only debate was whether he'd come to church or not. In the early days he did come most of the time. We both made friends, but we never had anyone over to our home."

Otis suddenly snorted in his chair, jerked his big head against the back of his chair and began to quietly snore.

"His brothers had of course married Kansas girls, so we saw a lot of them, but he liked having me to himself. I used to complain, but that did no good."

Foster stared into the fire. "I thought you were a happy couple."

"Oh, I think we are. We've made it work. I've gotten jobs now, have lots of friends. But he's always kept this place as his own little fort. So I think this was a step in the right direction. Bringing you here. It pleases me."

They sat in silence.

Foster put his whisky glass down, got up from his chair, and added two logs to the fire. The flames flared up.

"Anyway," she went on, "this is a good step for him. A big step. He seems to like you."

"He's a pretty likeable guy."

"Yes, he is. He took me to Germany to see my relatives last year. The first time ever. It's one reason we started trying to raise cattle, to save up money for the trip."

"That didn't work out."

"No, but we borrowed money to pay for the trip. That was a big step for both of us."

Foster nodded. They sat for a half hour and then Foster stoked the fire and Anastasia woke Otis and helped him stumble to bed.

+ + +

Foster stood alone near the north bedroom window. He had blown out Anastasia's candle on the guestroom dresser and now peered up at a vast array of stars. At least the snow had stopped. No one in the surrounding farms had electricity, so the stars shone with particular intensity. Beneath the starlight and the faint light of a crescent moon he could see the way the wind had carved the snowdrifts around the front-yard trees that stood naked, cold, and still. Though the bedroom door stood open to the dark hallway to attract the waning heat from the living room fireplace, it was icy now in the black room, and he felt within himself a stubborn loneliness that came to him out of the night, dropping down from the vast, silent voids between those distant stars, finding him here, standing alone. He wanted to leave. He wanted to get out and start walking again, but there was nothing for it but to slide under the heavy blankets between cold sheets and wait for his body to gradually warm his little cocoon.

+ + +

The third morning dawned clear and very cold. A bright light streamed through Foster's bedroom window. He swung his bare feet out of bed and dressed quickly in his own clothes which Anastasia had washed and dried that first afternoon. He looked at the icon of St. Isidore hung over the dresser: patron saint, Anastasia had told him, of farmers. T*hey needed a patron saint of cattle ranching.* He walked down the hallway in his own jeans, sweatshirt, jacket and boots into the living room.

Even with Otis feeding the fireplace constantly during waking hours, the bedrooms were shockingly cold and Otis had been worrying the water pipes were freezing. Before going to bed the night before, he had filled several buckets of water from the tub faucet to use in the kitchen and bathrooms. The central propane heating system required electricity to run the furnace fan, so it wasn't working at all. They had opened all the cabinet doors beneath the sinks in the kitchen, bedrooms, and bathrooms and Otis had gone into the basement and turned off the water, leaving all the water faucets open to drain the pipes.

The fire was burning brightly as Foster walked by it. He could see that Otis had set up a grill over the logs and there was a camper's coffee pot set over the flames. The fire took the edge off the cold but when Foster turned into the kitchen, Anastasia had her winter coat on and was shuffling about in wool socks and snowboots. She put on a baker's glove and went to the fire to retrieve the coffee pot. She poured him a cup of hot coffee and added cream.

Just then Otis pulled open the back door and stepped in, stomping his boots on a rug near the door. "Mercy!" he said, "Must be heading toward zero out there." He had gone out to pull down hay from the shed loft for Abraham and Sarah and had spent a half hour using a front-end loader attached to his tractor to push the snow from his driveway.

"Tried to chop the ice to get Abe and Sarah some water," he announced, "but nothin' doing. Froze solid. We need to heat up a pail of water and take it out there."

Foster said, "Don't cows eat snow when they're thirsty?"

"Sure they do, but they're my guests! I don't make you go out and eat snow do I? A little warm water might make 'em think I liked 'em." He grinned.

"They're his babies," Anastasia said.

"Not babies. In this weather, they're fellow soldiers. We've been together for over three years now. Young Abraham tells me to get my ass in gear when he don't get what he wants."

"Otie keeps a bushel of apples beside the back door," said Anastasia, "and when he runs out of apples, that bull will grunt and kick the side of the shed like we owe him. We need to sell that bull."

Otis looked at his wife and nodded. "Maybe so," he sighed. "Or maybe no. He don't do us much good without another cow and we can't afford one just yet."

She poured Otis a cup of coffee and added cream. "At least the snow's stopped," she said. "But I still want to go to church, Otie. It's Sunday, you know."

"Sunday?" he said. "I lost track of the days. My phone's lost its charge and we still ain't got electricity. And no way you're gettin' to church, Stasia, unless the snowplows make it by our place."

"I think the plows will be out and about, Otie. I expect in the next few hours we'll have an open highway. We've been through this before, and I'm sure they've been working all night."

"Well, you better start prayin', cause if they don't plow us out by ten o'clock, you're not makin' it to church. But if they make it here by then I'll take you. I don't want you drivin' yourself in this."

He looked at his watch. "Eight thirty it is. Time enough for breakfast."

Anastasia took a little wooden stool and placed it in front of the fire and used a black cast-iron frying pan and a metal spatula to fry eggs and bacon.

The conversation drifted to Foster's wife and her nursing profession. "Stasia here," said Otis, "wanted to be a nurse, but when we got here, she didn't know English good enough to take nursing courses. So she picked up whatever job came open in Holton. I think your first job was at that little Mexican restaurant. Then she had to start learnin' some Spanish, too, to talk to the cook. The owner knew English good, but the cook was straight out of some pueblo in Mexico and was learnin' English his own self. I remember one night . . . Hey! I do believe your prayers been answered, Stace. I hear the plow. You know what that means, Foster?"

Foster looked at Otis.

"You're goin' to church!. If I'm goin', you're goin'. I don't always make it, but I ain't lettin' Stasia here drive herself with the road only half plowed."

+ + +

The five or six miles to Holton had one lane cleared when they left home. Now and again, the truck tires would spin and they'd lose traction. Otis blamed it on the sleet that had come down before the snow. "Leaves a hard layer of ice 'neath the snow," he said.

Near town, the snowplow met them coming the other way, but no one else was on the highway. They drove up the snow-packed street and stopped before the church, a brick building with a steep roof and a brick tower surmounted by a high copper-colored steeple. There were a few cars and pickups parked along the street and in a parking lot, but not many.

Someone had shoveled off the sidewalks and front steps. Foster followed Otis and Anastasia up the steps and into the front door. Two rows of wooden pews led up to the altar set beneath a domed ceiling at the far end. Maybe thirty or forty people were scattered across the pews; a few families had even brought their children.

The three of them stepped into a pew near the back and sat down.

Having attended a Catholic funeral once, Foster remembered the getting up and sitting down, getting up and sitting down, getting up and kneeling that had marked that service.

A woman stood up next to the organ and announced the entrance song. A man began playing the piano, everyone rose to their feet, and a priest followed a boy carrying a tall crucifix up the central aisle. The priest was short and bald and robed in purple vestments.

Foster didn't pay much attention to the service; he was more interested in making sure he was standing when Otis and Anastasia were standing and sitting when they sat.

Several minutes into the service everyone stood again and sang something as the priest picked up a heavy red book and carried it above his bald head to the pulpit on their left. He stood beneath a painted wooden statue of Mary and her child that hung on the wall behind him. The priest read from the book, then everyone sat down but the priest. He was a young man, perhaps from the Philippines, but he spoke English without an accent.

He said that the Gospel reading for this the third Sunday of what he called Advent quoted Jesus' own words about the prophet and teacher John the Baptist. John, said the priest, was an ascetic who wore a camel-hair robe and leather belt while living in the desert regions east of Jerusalem. John was the son of a temple priest, so by rights he should have been serving as a priest of the temple in Jerusalem, but he had retreated to the desert where he survived on locusts and wild honey. In the centuries that followed, the priest said, many men fled the cities and lived as monks or hermits in the wilderness. He looked up. "You've heard of the Desert Fathers, right?"

He said that he had been reading a hymn by one of those ascetical Christian monks. This monk, he said, lived a thousand years ago near Constantinople in what is now Turkey. The priest looked down and began to read the hymn.

All Foster took in was that it kept repeating the word *come*. "Come true light, come eternal life, come hidden mystery," come this, come that, come the other thing. Something about a nameless treasure. After reading the hymn, the priest said something about how the Eastern churches sometimes try to help define God by defining what he is not. God has no beginning. No end. God is not limited by space or time. God is not a being like all created things, but is the source of being itself. How could we possibly define the *ineffable*. Foster noticed that he repeated that word: *ineffable*.

The priest lapsed into a story about his graduation from the University of Kansas with a degree in mathematics. About his increasing understanding at the time that his role in life was changing. That in spite of some emotional dryness, distractions, loss of focus on what he called 'the one necessity', he had begun to lean toward a new understanding of that necessity.

He went on but Foster suddenly noticed the long dark hair falling down the back of the barista Cindy's coat across the church. She sat on the far side of the aisle near the front and there was a wheelchair parked beside the pew. From what Foster could see, there was a child in the wheelchair. Her sibling? Her child?

The priest had finished his sermon and was walking back to his chair. He said something and everyone stood up and began reciting something.

Foster stepped into the aisle and left the church. He wasn't going to fall into a conversation with Anastasia, Otis, and Cindy in which she would find out that he was a relatively wealthy businessman while Cindy thought him homeless.

He pushed open the church door. The snow was blinding, the air frigid. He made his way to Otis's pickup, opened the back door, and slid into the seat. It was cold. Very cold.

He waited.

Twenty minutes or more later the church doors opened and people stepped into sunlight. Otis and Anastasia soon returned to the pickup and climbed in. "What the hell chased you out of there, Foster? You pissed off about something?" Otis said from the front seat.

Anastasia said nothing but glared at Otis.

Foster shrugged.

Driving home with them, Otis looked into the rearview mirror at Foster. Foster could see his smiling eyes.

"I used to tell my church-going buddies at the plant that there is no way you can describe God. Why do you even try? If he's up there, you ain't able to put him into words. How can anybody describe someone who's invisible and everywhere? Ain't that exactly what that little priest was sayin' this morning? So, Stasia, you see the little man agrees with *me*! What's the word he used? *Inexpressible. Indescribable.* Something like that."

Foster could see Anastasia shake her head. "You might not be able to describe God, husband, but he gave us 73 books in the Bible to help fill in the blanks."

"But what's the point if you can't describe what you're lookin' for? If God is so huge, he's bigger and smarter than a giant to a grasshopper, bigger than the sun to a candle, bigger than the universe to a speck of dust. Ain't that right?"

She said, "Maybe he speaks grasshopper to people like you so you can understand."

Otis grinned. "Hey, I like that! I do like that. That's what I need. The Grasshopper Gospel. Didn't that prophet he was jawin' about eat grasshoppers?"

When they reached home and stepped in the door, the lights had already come on and the furnace was running. Otis checked the thermostat and it had already risen to 50 degrees. He went to the basement and turned the water on, then moved from room to room turning the faucets off. "No leaks!" he announced when he returned to the kitchen. You got to check the drains too in times like this. I had a work buddy lived in a trailer house when his toilet drain froze up. Couldn't flush his shit. Now that's a fix nobody should have to deal with on a winter day. It was something like ten below zero when he crawled under his trailer with one a them torches and started trying to unthaw his toilet drain. Wouldn't you know it, the frozen drain exploded in his face! Said by the time he managed to crawl out, the shit had already froze in his beard. It was that cold. He had to drive to a gas station and use their restroom to clean off his face." He grinned.

"A fine story to tell just before lunch," said Anastasia.

"Well it's true! You know Gus Norton. Happened to him."

She was busy in the kitchen heating up spaghetti sauce, frying some hamburger and onions and mixing it all together with a few basil leaves. She set the pan to simmer. Otis took down a bottle of red wine as Anastasia boiled sticks of spaghetti. An hour later, they sat down for lunch.

Foster looked at Otis. "Was that the barista from the coffee shop I saw sitting up front in the church?"

"Oh, yeah. Cindy. That's Cindy all right. She lives with her mom a couple of blocks from the church. Her mom wasn't there this morning, so Cindy must have driven over with the boy. That's Cindy's kid in the wheelchair. Cerebral palsy. That's what he's got. Guess he had the umbilical cord wrapped around his baby neck when he was born. Pretty damned disabled. Can't even talk and has to be strapped in the wheelchair. But he smiles a lot."

"Her kid, you say?"

"Yep. She was always a good kid, but got to runnin' around with a real bastard when she was in high school and ended up havin' a kid, but she had the good sense not to marry the bastard. Real smart girl. Always wanted to go to college, but got strapped with a disabled kid."

Anastasia intervened. "She loves that child. She and her mother both. He's allergic to cow's milk so they have to feed him goat's milk, which isn't cheap. Somebody last summer gave the boy a taste of ice cream at the city park and he had an allergic reaction. They had to run him off to a Kansas City hospital and she and her mom spent three weeks with him in intensive care. They love that boy."

"So she doesn't go to college?"

Anastasia shook her head. "No. She wanted to, but it's all she and her mom can do to take care of the boy."

Foster returned to his spaghetti. "Who supports the family?"

Otis took a sip of wine. "Cindy's dad's long gone. I never knew the man, but the mom's got her own cleaning business. Cleans people's houses and a business or two, and when she's not working and can take over caring for the boy, Cindy works at the coffee shop. They got the week all mapped out so they can trade off."

Foster nodded.

After lunch, he said, "You know, folks, you've treated me right, better than right, better than I could ever expect, but now I think I need to get back home. My wife will wonder where I've gone and my Jessica girl will be asking for me."

Anastasia looked at him and smiled. "Otis, Foster needs a ride to the Missouri River. Near Atchison did you say? Take a chain and your four-wheel drive and pull him out of the snow if he needs it."

"Well," said Otis, scooting his chair back and standing, "I reckon the snowplows have reached K-4 Highway by now and K-4 should be good all the way to Atchison."

"And maybe," she added, "a jumper cable in case his battery's dead."

Otis put his big, rough hands on the back of his chair. "It's only been, what? Seven or eight days since you left your car? It should be all right. Should still have some fire left in that battery of yours."

"Otis," she said. "Those roads are icy, and maybe they haven't got the salt trucks out yet. You be careful out there."

"Will do, lady. Will do."

But a half hour after they left the house, they were back home. Twice Otis had lost steering in a sheet of ice, the truck swerving briefly into the roadside snowbanks left by the snow plows, catching the tires and almost jerking them off the road. Otis decided to try again the next day after the salt trucks had passed.

\+ + +

That night the house was warm, but Otis lit a fire anyway. He turned out the lights, shut off the television, and as before they sat around the fire and shared their lives. Anastasia brought out a bottle of wine, saying she didn't want Otie to fall asleep again drinking whisky, and the three of them talked long into the night.

\+ + +

The next morning dawned clear and still cold. Anastasia made them cinnamon rolls and fried eggs for breakfast and brewed a thermos of coffee to take with them. She came to the door to bid Foster goodbye.

"It's been wonderful getting to know you, Foster," she said. "Bring your wife and daughter to see us."

Foster gave her a hug and thanked her again, lifted his backpack, and Otis and Foster walked out the back door, through the mud room, and out to the truck again, loaded Foster's backpack in the back seat, and climbed in. Abraham, chewing hay, lifted his big head and watched them leave.

Otis had called Charlie at the plant to let him know he'd be late to work, but Charlie told him to take it easy and come when he could; lots of workers were still socked in along rural roads unplowed. Along the highway, salt trucks had passed at least once and in most places the ice had melted, but occasionally they hit a slick stretch of ice or packed snow.

"Foster, buckle up there. I ain't got no airbags in this old beast. I was drivin' through the Flint Hills south of here one early morning. A Sunday. I was just takin' a drive 'cause Stasia was in church. I came over a hill and there, smack dab in front of my face, was four cows on the highway directly in front of me. All out for a Sunday stroll. The airbags both went off, bang! Burned my cheek, but it probably saved my life. When I came to, one of them cows was standin' on the road with a broken back, its hind legs collapsed. Couldn't move. When the deputy sheriff showed up, he had to shoot the poor thing in the head. Anyway, I ain't never replaced the airbags. Used the insurance money to buy me that cow Hagar. So buckle up. These roads are a bit dicey."

The sun climbed over the eastern hills. Snow everywhere, the sun reflecting in their faces as they drove east. Otis was telling him a new story but his eyes and thoughts were on the passing landscape: miles of swept snow perfectly white, etched with inky lines of trees and the occasional home or farm packed in white. A vast snowscape of silent, empty fields stretching away to the passing horizons. The truck crossed a small creek overhung by grey trees, the stream a smooth white passageway of snow winding away through forest. He thought, as they drove on, of the hard ice beneath that snow and of the black water beneath the ice trickling slowly, little by little over pebbles, cold mud, and rocks on a long, long journey to the sea.

He watched several crows climb into the blue sky and glide into a stand of dark junipers. One landed in the bare branches of a cottonwood tree. He wished he could hear their calls.

A Song in Winter

Someone complaining . . . . . .Cursing . . . The hum of a heater fan . . . . . . A croaking groan . . . Talking, someone is talking . . . Hanging in the air, a nagging pain in his right shoulder. A crow calls, harsh repeated cawing somewhere near. . . Smell of blood.

He opens his eyes.

The windshield has shattered into a spectacular, jeweled pattern of sparkling lights. He stares at the colored lights: small prisms of light outlining each shattered piece, yet strangely fixed in place, each piece fitting the next like a puzzle. From below him, Otis is saying, "Foster, Foster! You got to wake up. I'm dying down here. Damn it to hell, you got to wake up and get us the fuck out of here. My phone's busted and you ain't got one."

Foster turns his head and looks down into the shadows of the pickup cab. Otis lies crushed between his broken side window and the driver's wheel. Foster sees blood on the big man's face and blood seeping from his matted grey hair. Blood is pooled on the broken side window beneath the man.

Foster sees that he himself is hanging from the seatbelt and the pain is in his right shoulder where the seatbelt holds him tight.

Snow covers half the windshield and lays a shadow across big Otis beneath him. Foster can't remember what happened beyond the fact that Otis had been driving him back to the Missouri River to retrieve the car he had hidden there more than a week ago. Hidden it there so he could leave everything for a week or two: wife, child, work, stress, distress and walk away. All of this comes quickly back to him, but he has no memory of the accident. The long winter hike with backpack settles into his mind. Away from Kansas City. Away to the rural backroads of northeast Kansas . . . away . . .

"Foster, God damn it! Get that window down and crawl out of there before I bleed to death! I can't move. I can't feel my legs. I'm cut up between my ribs. I do feel that!"

Foster slowly reaches for the button to open his window. It comes to him that the engine of the truck is still running, the heater fan, blowing. He presses the window button. It seems a miracle that the window slides easily down. Cold air enters. His left hand follows his seatbelt down to the seatbelt release. Finds it and pushes with his thumb. His body collapses onto Otis beneath him.

"Get the hell off me, man! I'm bleeding!" They lie there together in a jumbled heap. Otis is groaning. "Get the fuck off a me, man."

It comes to Foster that the truck must be lying at some kind of sharp angle on its left side in a snowbank. He reaches for the open window above him and pulls himself up toward the opening, but Otis grabs his leg that is trying to gain a toehold on the stem of the steering wheel. "No! Don't go yet. We're miles from Atchison, out in farm country. Unless you catch a quick ride, I'll be bled out before you get back. I can feel it, man. Soakin' my left side. I must have glass in my ribs." He coughs. "Damn it. Damn it to hell, Foster. I don't think I'm goin' to make it out of this one. Listen, you got to do me one big favor."

Foster feels the grip of the big man's hand on his ankle. "Otis. Of course. Sure. Of course, but let me pull myself out of here and get myself up to the highway."

"No! This is going to take a minute, but I got to do it."

Foster's left boot finds the wheel's stem and he pushes up, slides his back along the backrest of the seat, grabs the frame of the open window and pulls with his right arm. Pain! That shoulder. He shoves his left shoulder against the shattered windshield that glows in direct sunlight. He finds a position where he can prop his left shoulder against the jeweled windshield without lying on top of Otis. He gasps for air and begins to pant, trying to hold himself in place. "What is it, Otis?"

"Look, you know how religious my wife is. She's always tried to get me to listen to her, but I always laughed her off. Didn't even go with her to church much in recent years. But Foster . . . Foster." Foster hears him pause and take a deep breath. Foster thinks he might be sobbing, but he can't see his face from the awkward position he's in: one foot on the steering wheel stem, his right arm out the open window now, his armpit clamped to the side of the truck, his head twisted between windshield and side window, his left shoulder pressing against the shattered windshield.

"I'd tell you to bring me a priest, Foster. I knowed for years I did believe and ought to get the job done, but I liked playin' her along and leavin' it off till later. Anyway, I don't think you're goin' to find a priest today. So I got to make my confession now. I got to get this done before I croak."

"What? Otis. Otis, please! If you believe, you believe. I don't go in for that stuff. You don't need to confess anything to me." Foster grits his teeth and gasps. "You don't owe me anything. You don't have to confess anything to me. You know that!"

"I don't know that," comes the voice from below him.

Foster tries to push himself out the window. He gets his head and right shoulder out the window into the frigid air, but Otis grips his booted ankle and he will not let go.

"First off," comes the voice below him. "Tell my wife I'm real sorry for puttin' it off like I did. That was nasty, I know. I been thinkin' a lot about it these last three days you and me and her spent in the house waiting out the blizzard. So, go to her. Tell her I'm sorry. Then off to that little priest over there at St. Dominic's. Tell him everything I'm goin' to tell you now. Anastasia always said I had to go to confession and that's probably the main reason I never went through with the whole deal."

"Otis! I do not want to hear this. Let me go and I'll get up to the highway. I'll get you some help." He forces himself further out the window.

Foster can hear Otis sobbing there in the shadow of the snowbank. Crows are calling. The heater fan is blowing. still warming the cab even with the window open. Foster pushes himself up further, then jerks his leg free and hears Otis cry out, "No! Foster! You can't leave me like this." He is sobbing.

Foster manages to place his hands on the truck's door and push his body up. He wiggles out and falls head first into the snowdrift beside the truck. He rolls and jerks his head back out of the snow, pushing himself to his knees in the powdery snow. There's an intense pain in his right shoulder. He hears Otis calling. The crow in a nearby tree calls out three times, raises its wings and flies. Foster, on his knees in the snow, leans against the truck's open window and peers into the cab.

"My first major sin was getting a girl named Lucy pregnant my junior year in high school. I mean that's the first one that comes to mind. I know I was a helacious rebel to my poor mom and daddy at times. I sneaked out of the house and drank with the boys, but hell, everybody did that. Lucy. She's heavy on my conscience."

Foster is taking deep cold breaths from the exertion of fighting his way out of the pickup. He coughs and wipes snow from his face and spits. His shoulder throbs. "Otis. Cut it out! I don't want to hear it."

"Her dad made her get an abortion, Foster. He did. I've suffered that for forty years, man. I always said it was his fault, not mine, but hell, I'm the one got her pregnant. It was my kid too."

"Cut it out, Otis! Cut it out. Cut. Cut. Cut! I'm leaving to get you help."

"God damn it, Foster. I been helping you out for the last three days now, feedin' you, got you a bed, a ride out a there. You got to listen to me and pass it on to the little priest. This is maybe my last chance." He is sobbing again, his voice croaking.

On his knees, Foster feels the intense cold. He reaches down with his left hand and manages to zip up his jacket. The truck cabin is still relatively warm, the pickup's truck somehow still running, the fan blowing heat. Foster can still smell the blood in the cabin.

"Okay, Otis. Make it quick." He hears no one passing on the highway somewhere above them. Most people are no doubt still snowed in from the blizzard. He pulls his head out of the cabin window and looks for the highway. The truck is in some kind of forest, a grove of grey tree trunks and brush. Somewhere above, over the snowbank, must be the highway they'd been driving down. The truck lies on its driver's side, its back right wheel lifted in the air is still spinning.

"Otis, put the gears in park position. The tires are still spinning. It's going to take my head off if I try to crawl out of this."

"What? Don't crawl out of this. Not till I'm done, Foster."

"Otis, for God's sake put it in neutral or park or I'm leaving anyway."

He sees Otis's big hand move slowly to the gear shift and slam the gear into neutral. The tire's spinning begins slowing.

Otis is back to detailing his sins, going back to boyhood and wandering around through his life as a young soldier. Sometimes his voice catches and he sobs again. His voice is weaker. Now he's riveted on the sins of his work and married life. His lusts, anger, gossip with his buddies, his hatred of a certain man at work, his rejection of Anastasia's repeated requests to come with him to church. His making fun of her.

Foster knows he has to go. Must find help! What possible good does this endless list of griefs and sorrows do for this dying man? *Ridiculous!*

Crazy! Waiting is going to kill him! He slides down from the open window so he can crawl up the snowbank, but Otis notices the change in light when he leaves the open window.

"Foster!" he gasps. "Foster, I'm not done yet. Baptize me. Baptize me." Foster hears the words as he starts to crawl away on hands and knees through snow.

"Now! God damn you! Now!" The voice is strong again, Otis's old voice. "It'll only take a minute, Foster. You don't have to be a damned priest to baptize me. Anastasia told me that. You just got to say the fucking words. I got to go clean, Foster, clean! I got to . . ." He is sobbing again.

Foster stops. *If this isn't the stupidest damn thing I've done in my life! I swear to God. Stupid!* He turns and pulls himself up to the window again and puts his head in the window.

Otis jerks his head up and gasps, "Thank you, Foster! Thanks! Grab a handful of snow and get in here, Foster! Then you can skedaddle if you have to."

"Snow? What the hell for?"

"To baptize me, you shit head. You're not going to find running water in zero-degree weather."

Foster grabs some snow in his left hand and forces his shoulders back into the cab and slides down toward big Otis. "Make it quick, Otis. I think you're still bleeding. You've got to lie still so the bleeding will stop." He grabs the steering wheel stem with his right hand to prop himself. The pain in his right shoulder cuts like a knife, but he grits his teeth. His legs are sticking out of the window at a preposterous angle.

"All right, now," Otis breathes in deeply. "She told me you got to baptize me in the name of the Father, the Son, and the Holy Spirit. We don't have the candle and white cloth and all that shit. I've sat through a helluva lot a baptisms over the years, Foster, friends and neighbors' kids. Come on now. Slap me some God-damned snow on my head."

Foster is practically standing on his head, but his arm and throbbing shoulder hold him. He takes the snow in his left hand and places it on Otis' matted grey hair. There's blood on Otis' head. "All right, I baptize you. . . . There, that's done."

"No, God damn it! You got to say in the name of the Father, the Son, and the Holy Spirit! Do it right, you ass hole!"

"All right, all right." He's panting through gritted teeth. "I do it in the name of the Father, the Son, and the Holy what?"

"Not the Holy What, you fucker, the Holy Spirit."

"Holy Spirit. . . Satisfied now?"

"Hell yes!," says Otis. Foster can see that old grin return. Otis is actually grinning, there in the shadows. Then he coughs. Coughs again. "It's a done deal, Foster. A done deal! Now get to that little priest and pass him all my sins. Every one of the little bastards. I'm not holdin' nothin' back here, leastways, nothin' that comes to mind. That little priest there won't mind all this shit; he's used to it. Won't bother him much. He hears it all the time. While you're gone, I'll think up some more to add to the pile if I'm still kickin' when you get back, I can unload 'em then. It might take an excavator to get 'em all dumped out, but it's goin' to happen."

By the time he has said all this, Foster has forced his body back out of the window, grabbing the windshield shelf with his right hand and pushing back, but that kills his right shoulder, so he grabs the top of the seat with his wet and now bloody left hand and manages to shove himself back out the open window where he collapses again in the snow.

His right shoulder is hurt by all these gymnastics, but he manages to get up and peer again into the open window. "Otis. I'm going now. Lie still. As long as the truck's running you won't freeze to death. Stay still, man. I'll find help."

He turns, drops down on his hands and knees and crawls up through two feet of snow, ducking to avoid the slowly spinning tire, gets to his feet and starts to pull himself up the snowbank by grabbing broken bushes with his left hand till he can get his feet down, then he climbs knee deep through powder snow till he comes to a kind of crest and spots the grey line of the highway through the huge rut the truck blasted between trees when it slid off the highway and down through snow-filled brush where it slammed into a tree and rolled on its side. He follows the path broken by the truck till he staggers out onto the highway where he immediately slips and falls hard on his back.

He lies there stunned for a few seconds. Over the hum of the truck engine he can still hear the muffled voice of Otis still naming his sins, but the man is laughing now. Foster hears him call out, "It's a done deal, Foster, a done deal! Let Anastasia know that, Foster. By God you let her know that . . . and then there was that day I was pissed at Leroy and called him a . . ." his voice trails away.

Foster gets warily to his feet and steps carefully over the ice sheet till he finds snow-scraped asphalt. *If that was a baptism*, Foster thinks, *it has to be the worst baptism ever committed by any damn fool in history.*

He begins walking back the way they'd come. He remembers a house somewhere they passed not too long ago. He grabs his right arm with his left and begins hurrying along as best he can, trying to avoid the slick spots and some of the packed snow between the chest-high ridges the snowplows left. He crosses the bridge where he now remembers the snowy creek leading away through forest—that calm, white passage through brush and tall tree trunks—he remembers. He had wanted to walk away on that frozen creek, walk away . . . not return to his car, his phone, his work, his wife, his child.

He keeps listening for coming vehicles. The woods are silent.

Five minutes later he is walking fast and panting, emerging from forest. He wants to pray, but his mind reminds him that he has never been a believer, at least not since he was a boy running through a forest on the first full day of summer vacation, shouting 'Yes! Yes! Yes! Three months of freedom! Thank you God! Thank you God!' And he had meant it. Leaping over a log and crashing through a patch of tall nettles that stung his arms, yet still he shouted, 'Yes, God, Yes! Days and days and days of fishing and hunting rabbits. Time! I've got time!' he had shouted as he, the ten-year-old, leaped and ran and stumbled and shouted.

No time, he thinks, as he hurries along. *No time. Someone has to drive by and pick me up. This is exactly why prayer was invented. For these impossible situations.* He hurries on, pacing along the asphalt between those roadside ridges of snow. The sunlight dazzles him; he tries to keep his eyes down on the asphalt and packed snow of the highway to avoid slipping. Tries to push his pace. Panting. The icy cold rests like a weight over highway and field. It hurts his lungs to pant. His nose is cold, his ears freezing. He has left his hat and gloves in the truck.

The wide, snowy fields stand still in bright sunlight.

Fence posts with little white caps of snow stand deep in roadside drifts. There's not the breath of a breeze. A rusted old farm implement of some kind just beyond the barbed wire fence lies half buried in snow. Farther along a broken, one-wheeled trailer slants into a snowbank.

Glancing farther out, he sees a treeline and the grey hump of a forested hill. *How beautiful it all is. How beautiful! How can it be so beautiful? Overwhelming! The stillness. The grandeur!* He's surprised by that word.

It's the right god-damned word! he says fiercely. *But Otis is bleeding. Otis is dying. How can you take him like this? He was doing this for me. Three days of taking care of me, a total stranger. And now this drive . . . helping me out. He did it for me! Why are you killing the man? This makes zero sense. Zero sense. Zero.*

He stops. Panting. Panting. His lungs are aching. He puts his freezing fingers to his mouth and covers his nose, breathing and blowing into his hands. He is maybe a half mile from the bridge creek. The grey and patchy-white highway cuts a straight channel through snow toward a distant grove of trees. No cars. No trucks. *He's not going to make it if he keeps on bleeding. He's got to sit still. Sit still, Otis. For God's sake, sit still.* Foster's shoulder is throbbing wickedly. He begins jogging down the middle of the asphalt. Jogging. Panting. Holding his right arm with the left. Crying out for a car, a truck, a snowplow, "Something! Something! God damn it, bring me a car!"

Fifteen minutes later, he approaches a snow-capped mailbox. There must be a driveway, but it's still covered in snow. He can see by the smooth snow that no one has driven out or walked out to the mailbox. More likely, no one is even there. He keeps walking, but smells smoke. He stops and peers back through the grey tree trunks. A white house back there, and smoke from its chimney.

He turns back to the mailbox and tries to find the driveway on the other side of the snowplow ridge. He forces his way over the ridge and starts wading through the powdery snow. A rabbit bursts from brush and bounds away. He follows the little clumps of the rabbit's footprints set almost four or five feet apart. He forces his legs through the snow toward the house, keeping his eyes open for a dog.

But there is no dog, not even when he wades up the steps onto the snow-covered patio and up to the front door. He hears piano music. Christmas music.

Strange that it is two weeks before Christmas and he hasn't thought about Christmas once in the past week of hiking. Surely there were lights and tinsel on the storefronts of little Holton, Kansas where he had walked. Christmas candles and a tree in the coffee shop where he had met Otis for the first time. But he hadn't noticed. Come to think of it, there had been candles at Otis's and Anastasia's during the blizzard. Candles red and white on their dining room table. But he hadn't made the connection.

Here, there is a wreath on the front door of this two-story white frame house. A homemade wreath of twisted juniper branches and local pine cones, a red ribbon bow.

What's the song?

Someone playing a piano. Someone singing. A haunting, lovely song. What is it? His hands are aching, his ears numb. He blows on his fingers and reaches up to knock on the wooden door, with his left hand, but hesitates. What is the song? He listens. A thin, reedy voice is singing. "In the bleak midwinter, a stable place sufficed . . ." He can't catch the words, but he recalls it as a Christmas song far more beautiful than all the snappy, tinsled, frosty-the-snowman, red-nosed-reindeer, Santa-Claus jingles that dominate the shopworn December airwaves. His heart leans into the song, but Otis. Otis.

Foster pounds on the door.

The music evaporates.

There's a tapping sound inside.

Foster pounds on the door with his frozen fist.

He hears the door lock click. The knob turns. The door opens halfway. An old man with wispy, thinning hair and gold, wire-rim glasses stands there. He is dressed in grey slacks and a dark blue sweater. He leans on a wooden cane.

"Can I help you?"

"We wrecked on the highway maybe a mile east of here. My friend's dying."

The old man stands still as he absorbs this. Then he pulls the door wider and says, "Come on in. I'll get my phone." Using his cane, he taps his way hurriedly toward the black piano and grabs his cell phone. Foster steps into the living room, closes the front door and clutches his frozen fingers to his chest. He sees the man punch in the emergency numbers, then look up. In a second or two he looks down again and begins answering the operator's questions. Giving directions. He looks up. "Bad wreck?"

"Yes. They'll be able to see the tracks where the truck slid off the road. He's down there in the brush and trees maybe a mile east of here, maybe more. He's bleeding."

The man passes this information to the 911 operator.

Then he looks at Foster. "Okay. They're coming."

He adjusts his glasses and looks at Foster. "You're worn out. Freezing. The snow's all over your jeans Why don't you come over here to the fire and warm up some. Something wrong with that arm?"

"Probably. Jerked it pretty bad in the crash." Foster follows him toward the burning fireplace then stops. "I got to get back to my friend. He's hurt bad."

"Look, that's all we can do right now. We'll have to wait. What can you do but get him out of your car. Then what would you do?"

Foster thinks it over. *At least the heater's running. And there's no way I can pull big Otis out of that truck. He said he couldn't feel his legs. He might have a broken back or crushed nerves. He's better off staying put.* "Okay. I see your point." He sits down in an upholstered chair near the fire. His knees are numb, his ears and hands ache. He holds his hands out to the burning logs and rubs them together. He remembers the three days he spent with Otis and Anastasia sitting in front of their fire waiting for the storm to stop. Drinking whisky and wine in the evenings. Talking. Three evenings sitting before a good fire and talking. And here he is again. Sitting with a stranger before his fire.

"Can I get you some coffee?"

"I need to get back. Get back to my friend. He's hurt pretty bad."

"I can't drive you out. My car's two-wheel drive and it's in the garage. Can't even get the garage door open with all the snow banked up on the north side. I've got coffee made."

The fire flickers and burns, yellow and red flames setting coals aglow between three or four split logs. More split logs are stacked beside the stone fireplace.

Foster hears the old man shuffling about in his kitchen. He begins to notice the Christmas decorations: large pine cones on either end of the mantle over the fireplace. A fat red candle surrounded by juniper limbs cut and arranged on its center. Through an open door to the dining room, he sees an oak table decorated with a carved, wooden nativity set. Over on the piano there are several sheafs of music. A small Christmas tree with cloth and wooden decorations and white lights stands before the front living room window that faces the highway.

Foster is impatient. He stares out past the Christmas tree, through the tree trunks to the highway.

The man limps in through the dining room and into the living room with his cane in one hand and a white cup of coffee in the other.

"Do you need cream or sugar?"

"How long do you think before they get here?" Foster asks.

"Could be twenty, maybe thirty minutes with the roads the way they are."

Foster rubs at his shoulder with his left hand. Pushing at the wrenched muscles. He winces. "Seemed like more than 30 minutes to get here. Another 30 for them to get here," he didn't finish his thought.

He holds the cup of black coffee. Time ticks slowly. He sees an old-fashioned walnut clock on a shelf surrounded by ceramic figurines. The clock ticks. The man says little.

Finally, Foster says, "I can't stand the wait."

"They should be here in ten or fifteen by now," the man says.

Foster takes a deep breath. "Could you play me that song you were playing when I came up?"

The man, sitting in another upholstered chair near the fire, puts down his coffee cup. "What song was that?"

"I don't know. Some Christmas song. I need it. Something about bleak winter."

The man smiles. "Oh yes, Christina Rosetti's carol. It seemed the wrong carol for this morning and the right one at the same time."

Foster looks at the man.

"'In the bleak midwinter, frosty wind made moan.' Well, that's not quite right for this bright, sunlit day, so full of light, no wind." He smiles again. "But 'Snow had fallen snow on snow, snow on snow.' That's surely right for this day."

Foster nods but doesn't smile. He feels a deep longing within. A kind of pain the song triggered deep within, a pain competing with the pain in his shoulder. He looks back out the front window, past the little Christmas tree. No sign of movement along the highway. "So, you think you could play it for me? I'm going crazy sitting here waiting and waiting. I can't drink this coffee." He puts the cup down on the floor with his left hand.

"Well sure. I can play it." His voice is quiet. He takes his cane and pushes himself up from his upholstered chair, taps his way over to the piano, and sits down on the bench. He places his long, delicate fingers on the keys and begins a quiet, rippling introduction, lifts his fingers slightly, and begins to sing as he plays, that same reedy voice, yet strangely confident and competent: "In the bleak midwinter/ Frosty wind made moan,/ Earth stood hard as iron,/ Water like a stone; . . ."

The melody and words begin running like a mountain stream, swirling, through Foster's mind, falling into deeper pools, rushing him along, carrying him like a lost twig or leaf bobbing along in its strong but quiet current: "Snow had fallen, snow on snow,/ Snow on snow,/ In the bleak midwinter,/ Long ago. . . ." The fingers lift, and begin again with two chords: "Our God," then moves with a stronger cadence: "Heaven cannot hold Him/ Nor earth sustain;/ Heaven and earth shall flee away/ When He comes to reign./ In the bleak midwinter . . ." Then the words Foster had heard at the door: "A stable-place sufficed/ Lord God Almighty/ Jesus Christ. . . ." As beautiful a melody as Foster can remember, simple and moving, quiet and haunting, holding, carrying him in its quiet current. He sits entranced, lost to longing as he watches the thin old man in the wire-rim glasses lifting his chin and singing . . . . and after a few more moments, the song is over and the man turns to Foster and raises his greying eyebrows: "I'm more of a pianist than a singer. But I still love to sing."

"Please. One more time," Foster says. "Just once more. It quiets me."

The song returns to lift him again, carrying him like a quiet boy on a long-roped swing on a cold winter day, carrying him up to the horizon and swinging him back again. "'Enough for Him whom cherubim/ Worship night and day/ A breastful of milk, and a mangerful of hay;/ Enough for Him, whom angels/ Fall down before,/ The ox and ass and camel/ Which adore. . . ."

His fingers pause and begin again: "Angels and archangels/ May have gathered there . . ." Foster takes in the startling contrasts: bright angels and a cold, desolate stable, a high prince and a peasant mother, bitter winter and a mother's warmest love . . . When the old man presses the last notes, the harmonies fade. He looks again at Foster and sees the tears on Foster's cheeks. The old man bows his head, looking down at the black and white keys.

Later they sit at the dining room table waiting. The man smiles and points at the carved nativity scene at the center of the table. He doesn't comment, but Foster sees that it is another version of the song he sang.

The man adjusts his glasses and retrieves Foster's cup of coffee. He returns to the kitchen. Foster sees him pour the lukewarm coffee into the sink, pour him a hot cup, and return. He offers Foster cream. Foster nods his head. The man pours cream from a cardboard carton, pours himself some cream and returns the carton to the kitchen.

Foster takes a sip. Good, strong, hot coffee, but he's anxious again. They sit waiting for the ambulance.

"You retired?" Foster asks.

"Yes. Years ago. I used to be a music teacher at the high school. My wife taught English. We never made much money, but we were happy. Loved those kids. Never had any of our own."

"Your wife retired too?"

"She's two years gone," he says. He pushes his gold-rimmed glasses up his nose. "Two years one month come Christmas."

"I'm sorry. Did she love music too?"

He nods and peers down at his coffee.

Outside the dining room window the tree shadows lie like curving dark strokes of a watercolor on white. The few backyard trees are walled in by a thick line of dark pine trees. Beyond the black bristling trees, white fields.

Foster takes another sip and puts the cup down. "Look, I can't wait anymore. My friend must be dying. In the city it doesn't take this long for emergency services to arrive."

"They'll catch up to you on the road," the man says. "No sense trying to outrun them."

+ + +

They did.

Foster, still holding his shoulder had been jogging back up the tarmac when he heard the distant sirens. A white sheriff's SUV came first, blue lights flashing. Foster turned and waved frantically with his left arm. The SUV slowed and stopped. The ambulance was not far behind. Foster leaned down to the opening window. "The wreck's about a half mile up the road. You'll see it."

"Get in," the sheriff said.

Foster opened the door and slid in, not bothering to put on his seatbelt.

The sheriff stepped on the gas.

Foster pointed out the big ruts where the pickup had slid off the highway.

They scrambled down through the brush and snow. The sheriff tried to open the door, but couldn't lift it. He managed to climb onto the back side window of the pickup cab and jerk the door from above. The door came open an inch and one of the EMTs from the ambulance helped him open it. The engine was still running, the fan still blowing. Snow was melting off the shattered windshield near where Otis lay, but the sun had moved on and Otis lay crumpled in shadow, his eyes closed. The medic climbed into the open door and slid down into the cab, managing to sit himself on the steering wheel. He soon called out, "He's still with us."

It took them maybe fifteen minutes with straps and ropes to ease Otis up and out of the cab and get him positioned on a stretcher. He moaned, but didn't open his eyes. The left arm of his canvas coat was soaked in blood, his grey hair stiff with dried blood.

Foster wasn't much help; his shoulder ached badly. He tried to hold branches out of the way with his left arm and freezing fingers as they slid the stretcher up the snowbank and eventually into the ambulance.

+ + +

A week before Christmas, Anastasia called again. Otis wasn't walking yet, but she said that he was his old self. Telling the nurses crazy stories. Laughing at his own jokes. He was more than his old self, she said. A lot more. She thanked Foster again. Again, Foster didn't know what to say.

The priest from St. Dominic's had, of course, taken care of the confession, but he told Foster the man didn't need to be baptized again. Once was enough.

"So that was in fact a baptism?" Foster had asked the priest.

"Sounds like it," said the priest. "I talked to Otis about it and he was definitely sincere. You did the right thing for him out there; I know it wasn't easy. Otis won't stop laughing and telling people the story of his baptism. I expect he'll tell it the rest of his life."

+ + +

In early Spring, Foster took his wife and daughter to visit Otis and Anastasia. Otis was up and hobbling about the house by that time. The snow had all melted. New grass was springing up in the pasture behind the house. Across the pasture maple and cottonwood trees were in tiny leaf, but the oaks were still bare. Foster took his daughter to the back fence to show her Abraham and Sarah grazing now on the new grass. Anastasia, with her hair tied up in a flowered kerchief, followed them to the fence. There was a new calf grazing with the big bull and the cow. Foster turned to Anastasia. She smiled and said, "No, it's not Sarah's calf. Otis took some of the insurance money for the truck and bought us a little heifer. Saved money by buying an older pickup, so he had money left over for the calf."

Both Otis and Anastasia had firmly refused to take any payment from Foster for the three days he'd spent with them during the blizzard. "You don't pay for hospitality," Anastasia had insisted. Foster had looked at Otis, but he had just given him one of his big smiles. "She always wins," he said.

Jessica was fascinated by the calf, but Anastasia wouldn't let her cross the fence because "Males of the species," she said, "are absolutely unpredictable."

Foster caught Anastasia's knowing look and smiled.

Foster made his second contribution to Cindy the barista's family by way of the little priest at St. Dominic's. Foster intended to keep doing that; his graphic design studio was doing well. He told the priest not to tell Cindy, her mother, or anyone else where the money came from. "Make it a mystery," Foster told the priest. "I recall during that sermon you gave that you liked mysteries."

\+ + +

A few weeks later, Foster took his family to see the old, bespectacled man with the cane in the white house. His name was Bud Schermer. Foster had driven by the house, written down the address, and called the man the week before.

It was a shabby, cloudy, wind-torn afternoon when they drove up the driveway. Violets had appeared beneath the trees and bunches of daffodils here and there in the yard, white and red tulips on one side of the brick patio. A cool morning spitting rain, blowing their hair when they walked up the sidewalk to the porch. The old man knew from Foster's phone call when they were coming, so he met them at the door and welcomed them in.

All was quiet in the home. There were still sheafs of music on the polished black piano, but the decorations had changed. Christmas was long gone and Easter approached. A large white candle in a shallow crystal bowl rested on the black piano. Gold glass pebbles surrounded the candle. The fireplace had been cleaned out for the season, but when they made their way to the dining room table there was a large wicker basket of fresh flowers: white tulips, yellow daffodils, even a bunch of white and violet crocus.

They all had coffee together. This time Foster relaxed and sipped his coffee: rich and fragrant. Jessica had coffee too; she was a little offended by the old man's "Are you sure? It's pretty strong." She told him she was grown up enough now to drink coffee black like her father used to, but now that he was using cream, she would appreciate cream and maybe a little sugar. Foster's wife Carol had brought her special cinnamon and sugar scones.

After a few minutes of conversation, Jessica was bored and interrupted to ask Mr. Schermer if he had any quarters.

"Quarters? Coins?"

"My dad and I have this game going. We're trying to collect every state's quarter. We have thirty-nine of them. I have three of the regular quarters I can trade for any state quarters you might have. She placed them: one, two, three, on the oak table.

The old man fished around in his pocket and came up with several nickels and two quarters. One was from the state of Oklahoma, but she already had an Oklahoma; the other was a standard quarter with the eagle, so Jessica was disappointed.

"Wait," Mr. Schermer said. "Do you have Tennessee?"

Jessica looked at her dad, who shook his head no. She glanced at Mr. Schermer. "So do you have Tennessee?"

"Tennessee has a guitar, a trumpet, and a violin on it for their musical heritage. I had a jar of them I kept so when my students won any award at the state music festival every year, they'd have a little memento from their teacher. I think I still have a few in the jar." He got up, took his cane, and tapped his way back to his bedroom. He returned with a Tennessee. Jessica was delighted.

After coffee, of course, Foster asked their host to play the Christmas carol again.

Bud Schermer looked at Foster for a moment, but then got to his feet, took his cane and made his way to the piano. "It's Spring now," he said, "but a good song is always in season."

Foster, his wife, and Jessica followed him into the living room. Mr. Schermer told them to pull the chairs around and take their seats. He leaned his cane against the black, polished piano and took his place. He played the carol through once, with a light touch this time, in keeping with the season, then sang it as he had before.

Foster watched the face of his wife, and the face of Jessica. Jessica, her brown hair newly highlighted with streaks of blonde, seemed mildly interested, her dark eyes wide and curious; Carol's face was serious, as if she were listening to one of her patients in the doctor's office.

Foster knew they would not be moved as he had been that bright, still morning so filled with crisis, but he had told Carol about the experience, and it was clear she wanted to participate in what had moved him so. As Mr. Schermer sang, Foster's gaze turned and passed through the picture window. The Christmas tree with the cloth and wooden decorations was gone. The snow was long gone. Now the wind was gusting and blowing beneath a grey sky; the newly leafed branches were catching the wind and easing back and forth, the leaves dancing and fluttering.

Foster remembered that day long ago, sailing with his little brother down the coast of the Chesapeake Bay. On the third and last day of their journey, a strong southern breeze had filled the sky with low, scudding clouds and filled their sails . . . he could feel the fresh splash and rhythm of the waves . . . hear the seagulls crying . . . watch arctic turns skimming the air currents then suddenly dropping like small rocks to plunge into the waves, then flapping up into the wind to carry on their search . . . . His hand had been firmly on the rudder. He could feel it. He felt it now. That rudder so useless and aggravating the previous day when the wind had died, now guided them along as he tacked left and right and left again fighting the run of the wind, squinting against the salt spray, searching the long grey shoreline, choosing his way.

Now, for the first time in years, he could feel the rudder, though he knew it had been in his hand every day of his life. Now, at least, he seemed to be running with the wind, the sail filling, the ropes taut, the shoreline unfamiliar but fascinating.

www.ingramcontent.com/pod-product-compliance
Lightning Source LLC
LaVergne TN
LVHW020635100826
845148LV00012B/2191
* 9 7 9 8 3 8 5 2 6 9 0 7 5 *